TO PLAY
the Fox

TO PLAY the Fox

by M. S. CRAIG

DODD, MEAD & COMPANY
New York

Copyright © 1982 by M. S. Craig
All rights reserved
No part of this book may be reproduced in any form
without permission in writing from the publisher
Printed in the United States of America

1 2 3 4 5 6 7 8 9 10

Library of Congress Cataloging in Publication Data

Craig, M. S.
  To play the fox.

  I. Title.
PS3553.R226T6   813'.54   82-7442
ISBN 0-396-08099-5   AACR2

*To Corc
for his role as
Daedalus*

You must know then, that there are two methods of fighting, the one by law, the other by force: the first method is that of man, the second of beasts; but as the first method is often insufficient, one must have recourse to the second.

This was covertly taught to rulers by ancient writers, who relate how Achilles and many others of those ancient princes were given to Chiron the centaur to be brought up and educated under his discipline. The parable of this semi-animal, semi-human teacher is meant to indicate that a prince must know how to use both natures, and that the one without the other is not durable.

A prince being thus obliged to know well how to act as beast must imitate the fox and the lion, for the lion cannot protect himself from traps, and the fox cannot protect himself from wolves. One must therefore be a fox to recognise traps and a lion to frighten wolves.

Niccolò Machiavelli, *The Prince*

Part ONE

1

Le Chateau Frontenac, Quebec City, April 13

From the narrow window of his hotel room Igor watched the April rain leak from the mottled sky draped above the city. All right, by God. He had been summoned and he had come. He was in Quebec City just as ordered. Within an hour he would leave the dubious comfort of this room to walk along the Grande Allee where he was to meet Vladimir by the statue on the Parliament grounds. But why, why in the name of God?

He rocked back and forth on his heels, a small, stout man beginning to bald a little. He had hung his suit jacket on the desk chair. The droop of the coat's shoulders was identical to the slumping lines of his own body under the rumpled, striped shirt. His face, with its high, rounded forehead, bore an expression of almost comical sullenness.

With a tentative finger he probed at the flabby tissue just beneath his rib cage like a man blindly fingering for a hole in a dike. That transient pain had come again, the pain that had hit his belly when he received this summons from Vladimir, the Moscow chief of long-range clandestine operations.

For seven, almost eight, years he had reported to this man every six months, take a week or two. Always it had been the same. He would be summoned from his Washington, D.C., base to meet with his chief at one or another of Vladimir's favorite cities in the Western Hemisphere. Nothing could be more routine than these meetings where Igor delivered reports of field operations and received a batch of new assignments.

The very regularity of the meetings made this summons unsettling, bringing that searing pain to his gut. Only two months had passed since the last contact. The summons had been marked "urgent." Why in hell had they bothered to mark it urgent? Igor's consciousness of the slumbering power behind Vladimir's narrowed eyes made the most routine contact stink of urgency.

This time a lot more than Igor's consciousness was affected. The untimely summons had whipped his always sensitive constitution into a frenzy of dislocations. A headache had begun at once and before he had even started the long drive north under the bellying sky he began to suffer from a raspiness in the throat that promised hoarseness. The pain in his gut had become acute by the Canadian border. He tried to dismiss these symptoms as his body's rebellion against this unheard-of break in normal routine. By the time the rain began, just south of the city, the pain had become as steady as the linear drops slicing across his windshield.

He had a hernia. He didn't need any damned, patronizing doctor to make the diagnosis. He had a hiatus hernia like the chap at the bureau in Buenos Aires. He was a sick man being hauled on a long, dreary journey by the whimsy of that beastly Vladimir.

And beast Vladimir indeed was if a man can be judged by his externals. Vladimir was a man grossly obsessed by food, by drink and by cigars so vile that the stench of them hung about him like a vile miasma. His very words seemed to come only after being rolled about and moistened lasciviously before finding a shape in sound.

But to consider only the beast in Vladimir was to court danger. This unlikely exterior concealed a mind that was crisply ordered, ruthless and absolutely photographic. It was easy for Igor to picture Vladimir as mystic, his thick body humped in concentration as he played those long tobacco-stained fingers over the hidden network of his deep cover sources, receiving through the whorls of his flesh the pulse of intrigue drumming steadily beneath the lives of the world's nations.

Mystic or beast, Vladimir was in Quebec City and Igor's pain was unremitting as he stared from his hotel window into the jungle of chimney pipes and drains that sprouted from the angled roof of the old chateau. Had he said something wrong? Was it a faulty number, a forgotten detail that ballooned to importance only in the light of Vladimir's wider vision?

Some genetic aberration had gifted Vladimir with a mind that recorded with relentless accuracy each word he read or heard. His overweening vanity inspired him to flaunt this ability at tedious length. He was fulsome with Marx, of course, and a few of the more ancient classicists. His favorite source was Machiavelli.

"*The Prince*," he would begin ostentatiously, or, "from *The Discourses*." He would then quote, in the self-conscious phrasing of a sixteenth-century bureaucrat, some selection that bore only peripheral relevance to the matter at hand. It was a cheap intellectual pose and a deadly bore.

The sky was curdled beyond the window. The only use for such weather was catching colds. Igor wriggled his nose tentatively for signs of dryness.

But at least the hour was nearly at hand. He had little more time to sweat over what possible slip he might have made, what error of judgment had triggered this summons. He wondered idly if the agents who reported to him felt his kind of terror when he contacted them off schedule. They damned well better, he thought angrily, turning from the window to wrap himself against the weather. It behooved them to remember that clandestine operations were not child's play. A lot of college-type words like *détente* didn't change anything, not anything at all.

With his head cradled in an untidy nest of scarf, he left the hotel, ignoring the doorman's quizzical glance as he plunged into the pelting rain.

Only a few fugitive umbrellas hastened along Grande Allee as he passed the Ursuline Convent. The smell of wet dirt had been rinsed from the air to be replaced by a spongy scent of fungus and something vaguely herbal. Infrequent cars splashed by rapidly as if seeking refuge.

Only Vladimir, already standing studiously before the inscription on the moss-covered statue, seemed oblivious to the rain. He turned at Igor's approach and began to walk away briskly. In lieu of a greeting he announced, over his shoulder, "Fortunately, I have a car."

Vladimir drove silently along the shining streets. Sometimes during these meetings Vladimir engaged Igor in small talk of food or wine or mutual acquaintances. Since such informality could only be initiated by his chief, Igor rode in silence, breathing as shallowly as possible of the smoky air of the small rented car. This was a small defense against the poison of his companion's vice, which had clouded the windows of the car. The motor knocked mildly at the incline past the Battlement parks on the way to the Citadel. The seaway was dimpled with rain and the city on Igor's right was buried in the deepening murk.

Once parked, Vladimir stretched to withdraw a squat green cigar from his vest pocket. Igor shook his head at the proffered cigar, straining to keep himself from fingering his increasing pain.

In the flare of the lighter, the broad planes of Vladimir's face were thrown into relief. He had a peasant face, Igor thought, a narrow head for the size of his bones but without that heaviness of skull that so many of them had. Only his jaw was wide, a powerful vise strong enough to crush bones. He was from the north, Igor remembered, from Stroginskoye or maybe Sereda. Cavalry in World War II, decorated for bravery. He was no longer a young man. His dark hair showed no thinness, but around his ears glinted silver, curlier than the rest. His eyes were almost hidden in folds of flesh as he braced that forbidding jaw against the flame.

As the red glow of the cigar faded under its ash, Vladimir smiled over at him, a smile that Igor returned with sweaty relief.

"Helluva time to be in Quebec," Vladimir offered.

Igor shrugged, still smiling in spite of the churning in his belly that had begun with the fresh wave of smoke.

"There's a problem, of course," the chief went on. "It is something that surfaced in your last field reports." Then quickly, as if only at that moment conscious of Igor's tension, he smiled again. "It is nothing against you, you understand. It's just something that surfaced, something that needs handling quickly."

The man would get it out in his own time Igor knew, but his own head swam with questions as Vladimir studied the tip of his cigar.

"You're not going to like this," he warned, "but, as is my custom, I slipped in a couple of spot checks in that last group of assignments. These were simply reports I wanted through your agents on my own long-term deep-cover agents in your territory."

A prickle of annoyance rose in Igor's throat. Damned right he didn't like it. Even after clearing his throat his voice came out sounding querulous and complaining. "You may not understand how dangerous and expensive clandestine operations are in America."

"For money or fear I should do my own job halfway?" Vladimir challenged him. "You will recall, comrade, that Machiavelli himself in *The Discourses* talked of how dangerous long periods of time can be in the business of conspiracy." He paused, his eyes narrowing.

Igor groaned inwardly. Now he was in for a lecture on Machiavelli before Vladimir would get back to the reason for this meeting.

He seemed to be quoting, but at least his words had some relevance. "The dangers of conspiracy are manifold. The best conspiracy is that in which a minimum of time elapses between the plot and its execution. Involved as we are in a grand design that encompasses many years, possibly even generations, we can't idly presume that an agent put in place at one time will sustain his fervor until we have need of his services. It is only cottage wisdom to test the brew once in a while to see if it has survived its season."

Igor nodded meekly, his arm resting across the place where the pain was, in a vain hope that pressure might ease that agony.

"One of the agents I checked without your knowledge has been in place in America for twenty years. He has received small assignments from time to time, not so much for the value of what he obtains as to keep him conscious of his commitment. He has never shown any indication of failing allegiance, but it was time to test him again."

His smile was obviously designed to be winning. "Men are careless by nature, you know. A conspiracy can be discovered so casually, an imprudence, a dangerous intimacy. Machiavelli cites the case of Brutus . . . but enough of that. Let us only say that it was time to check and I am damned glad I did. Some instinct must have prompted me. The reports justify any risks that your agents might have taken."

Vladimir's voice trailed off as he drew on his cigar in short, avid puffs. Pale rings rose one after another to layer the top of the car.

"Then all was not well with this agent?" Igor pressed.

"All was not well," Vladimir echoed. "Let me review the problem that we face.

"The twenty-year man is Walter Heinemann, whose name you might recall from that last assignment. He is half Lithuanian through his mother, who inherited a goodly portion of land in her own country. She was one of those die-hard Lithuanian revolutionary women . . ." His voice drifted off, his mouth curling a little at some vagrant memory. He caught himself briskly and went on. "The boy's father was Prussian, German to the marrow, which didn't go down so well with his mate. When the Nazis marched into Vilna, the boy, Walter, came out our way. He was about seventeen, a good student who trained to be a good pilot. By the end of the war he had acquired a distinguished service record.

"You can guess what he found when he returned to Vilna: the city in ruins, his family deported, his lands despoiled, and his beloved mother dead. At that point he had the kind of hate that our service can use."

"But it was Germany that raped Vilna," Igor reminded him. "How did he end up in America?"

"Why not?" Vladimir countered. "To the faithful all capitalism is the same. On our orders he stayed in Vilna and got a degree in naval architecture. He still had this German name, you see. When the order came to deport all Germans east of the Oder Neisse, he was sent off with the rest. But he went with our orders."

"Orders," Igor prompted at last when Vladimir failed to emerge from his smoky silence.

"America," Vladimir said briskly. "He was sent to Sausalito in California and ordered to go deep and stay ready. Heinemann is fifty now, runs his own naval design company, is successful in local politics and possibly headed for power at the state level. He flies for recreation."

"This is a problem?" Igor asked, confused.

"It is from his sport of flying that the trouble has come. A few years back he bought a half interest in a crop-dusting company up in the Sacramento Valley, a firm called the Flying Mick, based in a little town called Blakeslea. It was a perfect setup. He got a tax advantage on his own plane, a specially adapted Stearman, and had access to cheap flying and the sense of being a part of the aviation scene. Heinemann is a charmer, a man who can get along with anyone. He's proved it by getting along with his partner, an Irishman called 'Mac' Maguire. They even made money to the point that expansion was feasible. They brought a third man into the company to help with this capital. We hope it is coincidence that the third man, the new partner, is Stanley Dobbs."

Igor shook his head. "That name means nothing to me."

"Nor should it," Vladimir assured him. "He's the son of Ukrainian immigrants into Ohio. Dobbs anglicized his name and went political at the University of Michigan. He first visited Russia as a student. He's what Americans call a volunteer."

"He can't possibly have the value of a man like Heinemann," Igor protested.

"Dobbs fell into his influence," the chief explained. "He married the only heir to a banker down the coast in Atherton. He runs that bank now, a bank that finances sophisticated electronic companies that have contracts with the American defense department. He has powerful friends and excellent access."

Igor felt his companion waiting. "Then surely one of them must be relocated," he decided aloud at last.

Vladimir's laugh was mirthless. "You know better than that. Those men have value only in place. The policy about contact between deep-cover agents is the problem. These men must not become known to each other in their roles with us. To do so would break cover. Neither man would have any value if he suspected his cover was in jeopardy."

Igor was struggling for some response that would not set his chief off again when the man turned genial. "In any case, that's not a problem you have to deal with. Such agents are not developed overnight. We lose such men with great reluctance. But it doesn't matter how accidental this connection between the two of them was; one of the men must go."

The low keening of a boat horn sounded from the seaway, breaking Igor's confused silence. Vladimir had said that the men had value only in place. Then he had said that one must go. It made no sense.

"This is the reason for my summoning you. You maintain a valuable and expensive field staff. You have openly boasted of their ability to use the most modern of scientific tools. Now we test this force of yours. We have complete summaries of these men's skills. We need thorough psychological studies of each man in order to decide which man lives and which man is expendable."

Vladimir's laugh came suddenly. "Your face is comical. Has America softened you so that you cannot face this alternative?" Before Igor could protest, he went on. "This is an attractive mission, comrade. How refreshing to choose between the good and the better instead of between the weak and the strong. But the outcome is vital and time is our enemy. This mission is to be completed within thirty days."

"You mean the psychological profiles must be finished," Igor suggested.

"I mean that only one of these men is to be alive at the end of thirty days," Vladimir corrected him.

At his words a slow ticking began in Igor's head. Thirty days ceased to be a month. It was a swift current of days whose minutes were already in transit.

"I give you a parable from the master, Machiavelli," Vladimir said cordially. "The master writes that in the old days it was the custom of princes to send their sons to a centaur to be educated. The centaur Chiron was half beast and half man. The lesson is that the survivor is the creature who uses both his human and his animal strengths." He waved his cigar stub with enthusiasm. "But not just any beast, Igor, not just any beast. All men think of themselves as lions. The master points out that a lion is helpless against traps. The best man is that one who has the strength of the lion but knows how to play the fox. Which is it, Igor, Heinemann or Dobbs? We must have still in our organization at the end of that thirty days the man who knows how to play the fox."

Igor sighed with relief as Vladimir rolled down the car window. The sweet, fresh air flooded his lungs as the cigar butt hissed in the roadside puddle. Vladimir did not speak again until he let Igor out of the car a few blocks from the chateau.

"Thirty days," he repeated genially as the car pulled away, fanning muddy spray across Igor's trousers.

The rain had stopped. Igor walked stiffly to relieve the continuing pain in his belly. The pain was softened by his walking. He picked up his pace. This was probably something a doctor could explain away in a few moments. He would have to see his physician anyway about the cold he was catching.

Lights bloomed along the streets. A young nun approached on the sidewalk. Her voluminous skirts were a little short, showing delicate ankles as trim as a deer's. She set her neat, rubber-clad feet down one before the other as if toeing an invisible line. Before she turned her face away from him he saw heavy fringed lashes half concealing her eyes. As she passed, her gloved hand caught her skirt closer to the line of her body to avoid his touch.

Thirty days. Fast, but not impossible. During that last handshake, the chief had pressed into his palm a flat, metal cigarette lighter. Once back in Washington he could examine the microfilm and set the mission rolling.

All men had flaws and even such wary men as hidden agents must move in a world where those flaws are on display. He had not vainly boasted of the skill of his agents. The decision was made before he reached the hotel. Only one agent was so well designed for this mission . . . good Communist upbringing, a distinguished degree in psychology and the talent to penetrate where other agents would find themselves shut out.

He shrugged. He had been a fool to let Vladimir's summons upset him so unduly. The man was exaggerating the complexity of the affair. All that Machiavellian blather was for nothing. "All men are flawed," he said to himself on that deserted street. Then he coughed and spat into the flowing gutter. "To play the fox, indeed."

The courtyard smelled springlike after the rain. It was April in Quebec, he reminded himself, seeing again the soft curve of the nun's cheek as she turned away. This city was only another Paris once removed by miles and three hundred years. If he were at home he would enjoy his Stolichnaya in which the dried lemon strips had been soaking these past days. Lacking that, perhaps the chateau stocked a vodka of some style. Perhaps they might even have some good hot Pertsovka to take the chill from his chest and deaden the pain in his belly.

Thirty days, after all, was an entire month.

2

The Flying Mick

Blakeslea, California, Sunday, April 14

Like a man who takes a sullen pride in his own mean origins, the town of Blakeslea flaunts the evidence of its humbler times. Old adobe business buildings still huddle around the Plaza, peering at progress through narrow windows. Those few ancient palm trees that escaped uprooting when the courthouse went up are cherished like decrepit ancestors who are not only self-supporting but have the grace to keep themselves tidy.

Away from the Plaza, humility disappears into carpenter gothic houses set back under alien trees. The driveways are bordered with flowers. The chaparral growth, once all the valley boasted, is now tended with nervous diligence against its sensitivity to water.

The landowners of Blakeslea had no trouble adjusting to the new affluence of moisture. They recognized the blue network of irrigation canals as a life system to bring fertility into their long-regretted investment in cheap acres of sand and cactus. Into that vitalized earth they set peach and Italian plum trees as far as the eye could see. Into the water itself they tossed the rice that was to burgeon into a multimillion-dollar business.

At the city-limits sign, Blake Avenue becomes a county-maintained road. Between looped wires braced against the wind, this highway rolls past canal and orchard, interrupted only by an occasional grove of live oak or the punctuation of standpipes.

Twenty miles south, an orange windsock flops desultorily above a metal hangar. Along the second hangar, parallel to the first, a fenced corridor contains the nervousness of guard dogs. They leap frantically to challenge anyone entering the baked dirt area where two trailers are parked on blocks among a fleet of trucks clustered at random around the lot.

Not until you are right on it can you see the airstrip itself, which is bordered by rows of prune trees growing up to the pebbled edge of the macadam. The air is heavy with a stench that resembles dead mice in a closed house. This smell of death is everywhere, a sulfuric memory of ancient eggs, the chemical pervasiveness of TEPP and fertilizer.

A hand-lettered sign identifies this as the Flying Mick. The same legend is imprinted on the sides of the trucks and along the closed faces of the hangars. The planes are parked beyond, a row of World War II Stearmans tied down against the wind. They look curiously maternal with lines of spraying equipment fastened to the back of their lower wings like rows of metal teats.

The phone inside Mac Maguire's blue trailer had begun to jangle a little before dawn. Mac had slept four hours. Rice season. At midnight he had put the last work order on the clipboard with the checklist of supplies for the pilots. Late rains had thrown the rice season two weeks behind. There was no catching up possible until the next winter, the next spring.

The four o'clock call had been a rancher fretting about his

scheduling. When Mac had stroked him down with assurances, the man had added a "Happy Easter, Mac," to his farewell.

Easter had hung in Mac's mind like the swinging of incense and the sputtering of candles. There had always been white lilies at the altar and Meg warm beside him, rising and kneeling as they watched their boy Toby jerk nervously in his acolyte's robes. God how long ago that seemed. Meg and he had been full into the fights that led to their separation by then. A woman had no right to make a man choose between herself and his work. "It's me or flying," she insisted, claiming that it was the only way they would make a "decent worker" out of Toby instead of a sky bum.

Well, he'd chosen flying and taken off, leaving her with the boy. And a hell of a lot of good it had done. In the heaviness of grief, he reached for another cigarette with the last one still tilted and smoking in the tray. Toby had chosen flying too and was dead, dead at twenty-one in a rotten Texas field.

He dug a deep breath from his lungs and stood up. There was no time for that, not for worrying about Meg nor grieving Toby. All five planes would be up this day with five full crews, flagmen and swampers with the posting checked against regulation. Evert had worked on the radio on truck three until dark set in and swore it was functioning.

Before the next call came, Mac had time to start hot water for coffee and scrape the stubble from his jaws, the extent of the obeisance he would make to this holy day. The trailer was just right for a man alone like he was now. When he had thought that maybe Toby might come and be a part of the business, he had toyed with building a house in town. He even had a lot a few miles south of the Plaza and three blocks off Blake Avenue. Now he thought of it as an investment that would pay back his taxes when the right sucker came along. He'd bought the first trailer for an office and pilot lounge only to realize that the damned things were perfect for himself too. They were like the cockpit of a plane, all function without frills. It was funny that Heinemann, being a pilot, didn't see it the same way.

"Good God, Mac," Walter had exploded, peering into the place, at the narrow bunk with a coverlet tight enough to pop a quarter, the lamp with its naked bulb, the single straight chair and the primitive cooking gear all out where a man could put his hands on it.

"I feel safer about the place being out here nights," Mac explained. "The dogs can't handle it all."

"Then hire a watchman." Heinemann had said. "You live like a monk."

"Grease monk?" Mac had parried, grinning at his friend.

There was no way he could explain how little his quarters meant to him. With Meg out of his life and Toby dead there was nothing left but the business. The business and the peace of the strip at night. His single lamp lured swaying pillars of gnats like the ones around the streetlamps back home when he and Meg had sat on the stoop in the cool of night. Here there were frogs too and crickets sawing away at summer. He wondered how Meg would react to the owl that haunted the prune orchard beyond the strip.

He had poured the boiling water over the brown dust in his mug and limped to the door with it before the second call came. The leg he had barely dragged from a downed trainer after his overseas hitch bothered worse these mornings, like an old wound growing new with time.

And son of a bitch, wouldn't you know that call had to come from his second partner, Stanley Dobbs? And like always, Dobbs was on the prod.

Mac listened silently while Stanley raved on, about overloading, about the maintenance schedule, about everything he could think to put his mouth on. Mac had an ugly instinct that a couple of the new pilots they had hired on were spying for Dobbs. Sometimes he even felt that the bastard himself was there, staring at him through the cracks of the hangar, just waiting for Mac to make a mistake so he could start clawing at him. Even that stupid plane of Dobbs's, that P-39 back in its special hangar, seemed poised, waiting.

Mac had reacted badly to Dobbs the first time he had walked onto the field. He was a big guy, handsomely dressed, with the same pale eyes Mac remembered from the Polack guys he had fought as a kid.

But he and Heinemann had made a mistake in expanding too fast, buying more planes than their profits would cover. The logical thing had been to let in a new partner and Dobbs had the money and the itch. Now it was Mac who had the itch, to knock hell out of Stanley Dobbs.

Instead he listened quietly, rubbing his fingertips on the calluses peeling from his right hand. A few months ago those calluses had been half an inch thick, tobacco-stained reminders of his hours on the stick of a Stearman, fighting the heavy control pressures of the beast, the slow rate of roll that kept a man's entire strength on the job. Some men used leather gloves against that pressure. Some even used both hands to hold the stick. Not Jim Maguire. But he hadn't been up since his son, Toby, hit the wires a month and a week past. Something hot in his belly melted his food into acid at the thought of the lift of a plane under him. The flesh under the calluses was as pink and soft as fear.

Aware of his silence, Dobbs began to yell. "You aren't man enough to run that whole show out there. Face up, Mac. It's outgrown you. We'll bring in a specialist."

"Specialist, hell," Mac shouted him down. "I'm the only one who can keep you in business here and don't forget it. You think your wife's money can buy you customers? There ain't a rancher in this valley that would touch you with a pole without me. I was here before you came, Dobbs, and mark this, I'll outlast you."

When he set the phone down he was trembling. It was bluff, pure Irish bluff. Sure he could still fly rings around most of these kids but he was slowing. He felt it in his game leg and his morning eyes, which took a while to focus. They were gaining on him and every day he stayed out of that sky their pace quickened. But he would be damned if he would let that broaddomed prick shove him out of his own shop even though the whole point of the business had been for Toby. When he and Meg had broke up he had found this one place to put the strength of his firm, sturdy life—into a crop-dusting business for Toby. Now Toby was gone and even the sky was slipping from him like the calluses off his palm. What in hell did it matter? He could take his money and move on.

The trailer window showed only the narrowest pale band of eastern light. Still barefooted but with his jumpsuit buttoned against the predawn chill, Mac carried his mug of coffee to the steps of the trailer to watch the coming of dawn. With the sun coming up at his back he never got to watch the whole show. Instead, he found a perverse pleasure in the fused light reflected against the western sky, turning the canals into brief lines of blood in the dark fields.

There was that strange thing about valley sunrises, every season came in its own style. Back in Pennsylvania when he and Meg had still been together, they used to have their coffee like this out on the back stoop talking low or not at all to keep from waking up Toby.

But those dawns hadn't been so much for color. The dark just seemed to be lifted, pressed back into the sky by light filling up the city, a thin grayness rising along its roof lines. You could easier tell dawn by sound than by color, the rustling of pigeons along the eaves, traffic sounds getting stronger as the street filled up with light.

He tossed the brown spray of the coffee on the baked earth and went inside to put his boots on. His men would be trickling in, ground crews and pilots readying for the day's long flight into darkness.

The call came as he started out the door. He knew right off that it was long distance from the singsong along the wires. He didn't recognize Meg's voice at first. The last time he had heard it had been when Toby died. Her voice had been stiff that time with her pain and she had refused to come. A woman refuse to come to her own son's funeral? What kind of a woman was that?

The aching hardness was gone from her voice now. Her tone was hesitant, almost fearful.

"James?" she asked. "Mac? Mac Maguire?"

"It's me," he replied, careful not to reveal what was suddenly thundering inside of him.

"It's me, Meg." Her voice was breathless, scared. Strange.

"Toby," she stammered, then paused. "You remember the Potter girl, Kathy?"

Damn the woman. She could never keep her tongue on a subject for two sentences running.

"I remember Kathy Potter," he lied. "Now get on with it. What was this about Toby?"

"Well. Kathy Potter. Toby." He could hear her swallow hard the way she did before galloping into talk with a panting spurt of new breath. "Kathy Potter had her baby, Toby's baby. It's a boy."

"What in the name of God are you talking about?" he exploded. "What's been going on back there?"

"Don't yell at me." Her tone turned cross. "You know I always cry when you yell at me."

"All right, Meg." He controlled his voice with difficulty. "Did he get married before he left for Texas or what?"

The singing silence. "Just what," she finally said meekly.

"They were just living together . . . you know. She went down there with him to Texas and they had a little place. After he . . . after he went down, she came back home. Now there's a baby."

A slow dawning rose in his mind. So that was why the little rotter had taken the job in Texas instead of coming to the Flying Mick where he belonged.

"I don't know a damned thing," he roared at her. "Son of a bitch, what kind of a screwed-up business is this? Living together? My Toby and some broad? Too damned smart to get hitched, I guess. Well let me tell you something, Meg Maguire. A girl like that will just tell you whose kid she is shelling out. If she did that with Toby, there might be any number of guys."

"It's Easter Sunday, James Maguire, and you go swearing like that at me." She was crying now, not loud but those soft breathless sobs that took forever to get stopped. "Kathy's not a bad girl whatever you say. She's maybe silly, but Toby was too. But the baby is Toby's, Mac, whatever you say. She came back from Texas carrying it and . . . well, Mac, he looks just like Toby, jug ears and all."

Mac gripped the table with his free hand, feeling the cutting edge of those peeling calluses press against the tender new flesh underneath. It wasn't that he was thinking. It was more that everything was boiling inside him, wordless and angry. A man does his best. He marries in good faith and fights for his marriage and his wife and a kid. He gives up a lot too, by God, a lot of peace, a lot of room. Okay, he lost that one. He lost Meg and then the boy. All there was left was a little chunk of real estate and something to make a living with. And peace. Not much peace but enough to hang on for. Then he gets this.

"Okay, okay, Meg," he said carefully. "Now you've told me. Kathy Potter shacked up with Toby and now she has his kid."

"Is that all?" she asked, still breathing unevenly.

"You got more on your mind?" he countered.

"She's going to give it away."

He caught a deeper breath. "So, it's her baby," he reminded her.

"But Mac," she protested. "He's our grandson."

"He might have been our grandson," he told her. What in hell was he hanging onto so hard? His freedom? His peace? Or was it just the deep hurt of Toby dead and still changeable by a few words across a bad connection on a long-distance phone?

"So what's on your mind?" he pressed again.

"I'm not going to let him go," she said breathlessly, still on the edge of crying.

He couldn't even see her as she spoke. She had given up the place they had shared because it cost too much. He didn't know what phone she stood by, her head ducked that way she did with the receiver tight in both hands.

"Whatever you say, Meg," he told her flatly. "Whatever you say."

There was a click and then the dial tone. She had hung up on him.

He stared at the phone a long minute before slamming it into its cradle. He felt as if he were swelling, outgrowing his own skin and the walls of the trailer around him. He wanted to kick the world in the ass, knock wide holes in the walls of the prison he felt closing around his shoulders. He balled his fist and swept his arm across the table, clearing it at one stroke. Mug, spoon, the telephone, the square bottle of instant coffee hit the floor with a crash. The damned telephone started to chatter again, repeating a recording over and over until it was replaced by a high, shrill hum.

Mac sat down heavily, staring at the chaos on the floor. Outside, his men were hailing each other. They would lift those clipboards down and start another day of flying. But only after running, each man in his head, that precise checklist that might make the difference between life and death, his own.

God, for a neat printed sheet to instruct a man about the kind of flak Meg had just thrown him. Life or death in life, not such a great choice. He couldn't remember his first fight with Meg about flying, but he could sure remember his last. At first he had really had to hustle money to send it back to her and the kid. He figured she couldn't help it that she was born with a tongue like a whiplash and Toby, being just a tad, was caught between them.

There hadn't been much money to send in the beginning. Crop-dusting was a new thing. You had to sell the idea before you could sell the flight time. But playing it close and biding his time had paid off. When he bought his first plane he'd taken an option on this land and planted those prune trees, figuring he could pay taxes with prunes if all else failed.

The company hadn't so much flown as limped those first few years. He cleared the land with a rented dozer, running the machine at night with its headlights probing the jackrabbits from the stubborn grass. The strip was dirt but you could land on it during the dry season. It was two years before he even put a crapper in. Then came the shop and the mechanic, Evert, who'd stayed all these years.

If it hadn't been for Toby he would have let the business grow at its own rate. Instead he took in Walter Heinemann as a partner. The planes went from two to four and the truck fleet up to six. The next plunge was the one they shouldn't have taken. Dobbs had driven a hard bargain for the capital he brought in. There was that stupid extra hangar just to house that damned P-39 of Dobbs's. Then, of course, they had to tear out bearing prune trees to lengthen the runway so he could take the thing in and out.

Heinemann's plane was there too, but that was different. He hauled that old Stearman in on a flatbed and announced it would be the company plane. Mac was skeptical even when he and Evert were cleaning the thing up and getting it freshly cowled. When the paint was on with that FLYING MICK blazoned on the side, Mac was more pleased than he wanted anyone to know. The Mick had an air speed of 170 and handled like a baby buggy. They used it for checking out new pilots, but what Mac liked best was watching Heinemann put that baby through her paces. That 450 engine never coughed at anything he threw at it, and the air show down at Reno didn't hold a flare to what that Mick did to the sky.

All for Toby. Then the little snort came back from service and went off to Texas. That was when Meg started sending the checks back. He didn't need to ask why she did that. She was telling him she didn't need him. With Toby gone, there was no connection left between them at all.

"Okay," he had said. "That's how you want it, okay."

He had quit going by to look at his lot, which he'd bought to put Toby's house on. He'd quit doing everything but fight to hang on to his company in spite of that Dobbs. And get back up in the air. Let Meg do what she damned pleased. Evert liked Heinemann. Because the Stearman was Heinemann's plane, Evert saw that she was greased and gassed and ready to go when Heinemann got the urge. That's what he'd do, take out that MICK, as Heinemann had ordered lettered on the side, and have himself a fly.

He heard the metallic grind of the hangar door being shoved open. The dogs were barking their welcome at the crewmen.

"Nobody's dragging me down that road again," he told the telephone, which had subsided to a low, petulant humming. He set it back in its cradle and pushed open the door, bracing himself at the top of the stairs before plunging into the frenzy of the day.

Juan, kneeling by truck four, grinned up at him, his face radiant.

"*Buenos dias*, Meester Mac," he called. "Hoppy Easter!"

3

Walter Heinemann

Sausalito, California, Easter, April 14

The irritation that had begun with Stan Dobbs's call began to ease a little as Walter Heinemann swung his Porsche onto Highway 101 going north. The morning was foul, with sea fog blanketing the headlands and trailing sensuously into Tennessee Valley.

Without enough sun to enjoy sailing and too much wind for flying, he might as well spend his day mediating another squabble between his partners, Stanley Dobbs and Mac Maguire.

Stan Dobbs was a mystery to him. What in hell did the man want? My God, he had money, position, a handsome family, including that daughter, Gretchen, whom he clearly adored. He was even charming in a rough-cut, primitive way. Walter had thought Dobbs insisted on buying into the Flying Mick as a tax shelter for his flying and whatever growth it might yield. Instead, Stan had been on the prod about Mac from day one.

God knows he didn't run his bank like that or he'd be out on the street with a tray of apples.

After the Marin traffic, Highway 80 seemed deserted. But then it was Easter Sunday morning. Dobbs had reminded him of that during his complaint over the phone.

"We've got to replace Mac with a new manager," Dobbs had stormed. "That place is in a hell of a mess."

"That's not the way the company is set up," Walter reminded him. "I put up a third of the capital, you put up a third and Mac's third comes from his land and equipment and his functioning as manager."

"Hell, I remember our deal," Dobbs said. "I'm even desperate enough to make a three-way split on profit . . . straight out, to get a decent manager here. Mac's got to go. I told him so this morning and the stubborn Irish—"

"I'll talk to him," Walter promised. "Try to cool down."

"I'd go myself," Dobbs muttered, "if it wasn't Easter. Ginger has a big party for a visiting aunt staying over."

Walter sighed, not envious of the day that Stan must face. But the pressure of Dobbs's private life notwithstanding, as a partner Stanley Dobbs was more trouble than his money was worth.

The last fight between them had been about Mac overloading the dusters. Dobbs had been hysterically certain that an FAA spot-check would catch Mac's Stearmans carrying more weight than was allowed. It had taken Walter two good days to get the two of them backed away. The argument hadn't been open and shut. Dobbs was justified in his concern over FAA regulations but Mac had his side too. Mac had to keep the shop profitable and the customers happy. What Dobbs couldn't seem to realize was that the business rested on the support of the valley ranchers. They trusted Mac and he might sometimes bend the rules to keep them happy.

This time Dobbs was taking after Mac personally, making accusations about negligence and personnel management. Walter couldn't deny that Mac had changed in the weeks since the death of his son, Toby, but a man had to be given time.

The fact that Mac had any life but the company came as a shock to Walter. He'd seen a faded snapshot of a young woman with a child on her hip among the clutter on Mac's desk without it really registering.

The call from Mac had come late in February, maybe early March.

"I gotta make a trip," Mac had said. "I can trust the shop to Evert, but I wanted you to know."

"Sure thing," Walter had agreed. "Be gone long?"

"A day, maybe three," Mac replied. "Whatever it takes to bury my son."

There had been nothing to respond. Jesus.

Mac had spoken into his silence. "Texas. He hit the wires in a duster in Texas."

"When are you leaving?"

"Today sometime," Mac said. "First I got to get a plane."

"Wait for me," Walter said. "I've got a plane."

He had hung up against Mac's protestations and handed his work to Curtis, his assistant. When he set down at the Flying Mick in the rented Cessna, Mac couldn't believe Walter was insisting on flying him down.

"You navigate, I fly," Walter told him. "This is one of those things a man doesn't do alone."

As rough as those three days were on Mac, they were good for him too. Legends always rise from the ashes of dead pilots. Whether the legends are good or bad, the pilot comes off as a little larger than life by the very nature of the passing. The stories on Toby were all good. Walter watched Mac listen to those Texans talk about his son in their lazy, distorted speech, heard them describe how Toby had handled a plane like a fractious woman, had imbued the deadly monotony of dusting with high adventure.

"In a fucking football helmet," one pilot exclaimed to Mac.

"That bucktoothed, jug-eared little bastard worked the sky like a hawk in a fucking football helmet."

"How does a pilot hit a wire like that?" a reporter asked.

"How do you stub your goddamned toe?" the chief pilot countered.

The boy had a mother named Meg. Walter leaned outside the telephone booth while Mac jerked himself back and forth in conversation with her. He had gone in there soft and come out tight-faced, looking every day of his forty-odd years.

A lot of Mac's great wit bled from him then. The songs he hummed in the hangar fell into silence. For a few weeks Walter had been almost grateful for the antagonism Mac felt for Dobbs. A little hate is better than no feeling at all.

And give him credit, Dobbs eased up for a while, forced back by the black magnitude of the Irishman's grief. But now he was bitching again.

"He's giving the pilots weebies," Dobbs insisted.

"Pilots always bitch," Walter reminded him.

"Not like this," Dobbs countered. "He's cracking up, I tell you. He's pissed off at any man who stays alive with his own kid dead. I mentioned putting a new guy in to run the place and he threatened me. He's overscheduling those men, tightening their runs right into darkness and overweighting the buggies just like before. He's not indispensable, you know."

Dobbs was wrong there. Mac was indispensable. There was no way they could pull into the black this season without Mac. The Flying Mick wasn't the only dusting shop in the valley. Just let those ranchers discover that some city banker had pushed Mac out of his own shop and those Stearmans would be gathering another sort of dust on the strip.

Walter eased his Porsche off Highway 80 at the Blakeslea turnoff. Slowing for the turn he saw the girl.

She was frail and tall and stood with her feet too far apart as if to root herself, however temporarily, in the earth. These women were so identical that they startled him. Without obvious defect they missed attractiveness by a turn of spirit he couldn't pin down. Their sun-darkened faces were narrowed by falls of straight dark hair, their clothes random and ill assembled. This one had nondescript eyes that held his gaze wistfully as if he might have something secret and healing to impart.

That same gaze made him conscious of the Porsche's polished hood, the elegance of the knit he wore, and the thickness of currency in the Italian leather wallet against his hip.

A sense of *déjà vu* forced his eyes away and his foot down on the accelerator. She was one of so many along so many roads in so many countries. They fused in his mind, this world of refugees, these armies of the uprooted, moving along alien roads, shuffling toward nowhere.

He seemed to have spent his life riding by where they stood. In Russia, during the war and after, the bandaged and embittered fleeing shell crater and occupation, fearing the unknown less than the remembered. They walked as she walked, stared as she stared. Even the clothing was the same, bulky and dark, so thoroughly concealing the body within that they seem discarded bundles conjured to a pained life.

But at least the war refugees made sense. Americans were different. What insane torment drew them from bourgeois beds to this exile? Could they be dimly conscious of the guilt of their blood-stained society? Was this what they were fleeing?

She was a dark staring post in his rearview mirror. They thought themselves revolutionaries. They were simply refuse, the flotsam and jetsam from the swirling passage of capitalism. They could be used and discarded, even destroyed, without compunction.

Revolution, the last glittering fantasy of the immature. Thank God all that was behind him. The realities of life had it all over the wildest dreams a man could host. A precise man, wedded to perfection, he took pride in his own painstaking documentation of ship movements, his intimate knowledge of the ports of the bay. He had had assignments over the years. His tour of the new atomic submarine had been easily arranged. The report he had filed on its jet-lift system was well enough delineated for a student's understanding. Every assignment had been fulfilled perfectly and promptly and each had brought a boyish lift of delight.

He knew how vulnerable he was. If he had ever entertained the idea of defecting, which God knows he hadn't, their hold was absolute by their evidence of his illegal acts. This only added an extra level of enjoyment, that faint prickling of the tissue that is wedded to danger. Not the steepest Sierra slope, not the swiftest sailboat, not even the most breathtaking aerial maneuver could touch that level of excitement. He cherished the blur, the giddiness of threatened blackout, the green throat of nausea. Not booze, not women, not even negative G's brought the exhilaration of a mission accomplished against a system that had destroyed his world.

Red-tailed hawks were hunting in the valley. They barely skimmed the fields, their wings tilting the deep, even turns. The wind was vaguely sweet from the blooming orchards that checkered the valley. And Mac Maguire and Stan Dobbs were at it again, a problem of his own making.

Yet who would have guessed that big, genial banker would turn out to be such a handful in a business setting?

He had missed the clue that was there from the first. Hell, any man who would own and fly a P-39 for fun either had the world's strongest death wish or was certifiably insane.

He first saw Dobbs and his plane at the Watsonville air show. He'd watched the hot little fighter touch down and start a desperate struggle to stop before the runway did, a sweaty, jarring contest that came with every landing in a P-39. He had felt his own toes cramp and wondered who in hell would do that for fun.

Drawn to where the craft was tied down, he approached it almost tentatively. A host of memories flowed over him as he neared the cigar-shaped beast. He hadn't touched a P-39 since the war, certainly not in the twenty years he had been in America. Yet he could still feel the incredible grind of that drive shaft between his legs, the racketing thunder of that Allison motor poised at his butt, and that damned independent right wing that dipped perilously if you tried to stall the beast with its garbage out.

"The flying coffin" they had called it. God only knew how many of his comrades had dug their graves in P-39s. The Americans called them Lend-Lease. The pilots had their own version. "They lend us the plane and we lease six feet of fresh dirt." His mind veered from Yuri, the cocky kid of Kiev who had the best tenor in the barracks. But Yuri couldn't believe he couldn't shove in the top rudder and pull back on the stick to tighten a turn on an Aircobra. Yuri died young and wet from Cobra poison.

The man who interrupted Walter's revery had strolled over with a wide grin. It registered on Walter that a man of his size had to put on that Cobra of his with a shoehorn. His tailoring, even in sport clothes, suggested that he could have that tool made of gold if he wanted it. He almost boyishly relished Walter's interest.

There had been an exchange of names and some spiritless beer in cardboard glasses and fliers' bull that finally got around to each man's business.

"A ship designer," Dobbs had repeated with amused interest. "That's a sport I've never been drawn to. Those damned boats must cost as much as planes, without the kicks."

"And they are even tougher to shelter," Walter agreed.

"So how can you tax-shelter a plane?" Dobbs asked, glancing at his own plane. "Outside of a little break on company travel or letting it out for student training?"

As he listened to Walter explain the Flying Mick, the cipher signs came up behind his eyes and the numbers clicked almost visibly behind the pale, broad forehead.

It had been natural enough when, a year later, he and Mac

found themselves strapped for cash for him to pull out the card that Stanley Dobbs had pressed on him. He had gone to negotiate a loan only to have Dobbs offer a deal that neither he nor Mac had character enough to resist. Of such had this uneasy partnership been formed.

Walter hadn't figured on the men's instant aversion to each other, nor to Mac's fury when his pampered prune orchard had to be truncated to extend the strip for the P-39 to land. Even the hangar that Dobbs had built with his own money grated on Mac. He sighed. Mediating took time, but it was better than an open break in a season when even the sky seemed against them.

A Stearman lifted off the field at Walter's approach. He watched its perfect curve as it angled toward a distant field. He smiled. God, how he loved those little biplanes. It was oddly satisfying that a machine designed to work so efficiently could still resemble a giant dragonfly in flight. Sending an insect after the insects, he thought wryly. Mechanized cannibalism at its pragmatic best.

Still smiling, he parked the Porsche in the shadow of Mac's trailer and circled the guard dogs in search of Mac.

4

Stanley Dobbs

Atherton, California. Easter, April 14

As Stanley Dobbs replaced the receiver of his phone his mind retained not so much the sound of Walter Heinemann's faintly accented voice as its tone.

Patronizing. That's what Walter's tone had been, patronizing. Under any other conditions that tone would have made him as mad as hell. In this case, it only brought a grin. So Walter had decided he was to be humored in his battle to unseat Mac Maguire from his management of the Flying Mick. This was better than Walter locking in stubbornly against him. As long as Walter kept trying to humor him, there was a little give here or there.

While Mac had been an open book, Heinemann himself was not easy to read, and certainly not to predict. For all his easy charm, Heinemann's style veered a little toward the cynical and his eyes showed practice in waiting. And his weird life, designing yachts for nit-picking rich men, back and forth to that miserable steaming valley and a solitary apartment. Where were the man's natural appetites? The wine, the women, the song?

Dobbs chuckled as he tugged the pull that let a wash of brilliant light in through his study windows. The view beyond was almost blinding in its brilliance. He had thought Ginny insane when she had planned the entire pool area in that pale blue and white. What had sounded like total cliché had come off breathtaking, water and sky blending against the rich green of the grove beyond. His son, Lafe, was reading—what else?—in a poolside chair, while Gretchen, her boyish body already bronzed with spring, twisted and dived and rose again to the board. Old Mother Nature had sure screwed that one up. Lafe would have been unobtrusive as a girl, maybe even appealing, a slender pale-skinned kid with dreaming eyes and quick emotional responses. Then there was Gretchen. He grinned, watching her toss her hair back like a spaniel as she rose to the pool rim with a thrust of those firm arms. What a man she would have made, gutsy as hell, her fine legs always scarred from soccer or some contest. The animal vitality in her face was a lamp in full sun as she saw him and thumbed her nose in his direction.

He watched Ginny set the poolside table, flourishing a great circle of pale yellow linen, letting it fall like a dancer's skirts to the floor. Her Aunt Iris, lifting and setting her cork-soled sandals choppily, came from the house carrying the centerpiece, a massive painted basket crammed with painted eggs and chocolate animals from See's. Easter.

He turned away shaking his head. It was wild, insane.

Easter began at early mass in a church cold from the night, so cold that the smoke from candles and the breath of worshipers mingled in a misty cloud of prayer. You stumbled home on cold feet for the feast set out on the kitchen table.

There was vodka, a little or a lot according to the money. As a child he had been told that his father's bosses celebrated

Easter with whole hams baked inside crusts and suckling pigs roasted on spits. Their own feast was kielbasa splitting from its skin so that globules of garlic-rich fat thrust from its innards like emerging rice grains, this with his mother's black bread and painted eggs.

Instead of a heaping basket the table was trimmed with his mother's kulich, properly blessed, its white frosting marked by XB and its top trimmed with plastic flowers from Woolworth's that his mother stored away from one Easter to the next.

Maybe that was Walter Heinemann's problem. Maybe he had never lived poor enough to appreciate what a lot of fun money could be. It was strange how much imagination it took to enjoy yourself wholly. It was so cursedly easy to stay in a rut and not cut your head free for bigger things.

God only knew what lengths he would have to go to to spice up his own life if it weren't for his connection with Vladimir. And he could take little enough credit for that, if he was honest. If his father had stayed out of prison and his mother had lived, he might be punching holes in an auto assembly line today, leaning on a bar rail and glaring at Irishmen like the old man before him.

But his dad had killed a man for a lousy two hundred dollars, ending up with his wife crying at him through the bars on visiting day for the rest of her life. She didn't understand why he robbed or why he had killed; she only understood that the pay envelopes no longer kept coming and the credit stopped at the corner market and no doctor was interested in her cough without money.

He had entered Michigan on scholarship two months after her funeral. The student trip to Russia had come with him still aching from his memory of her death. Liking what he saw, the onion-domed cities and streets full of heavy-boned faces like his own, he was ready to take the step past tavern discussions of Marx and Engel, and he did.

They had received him eagerly enough, congratulating him

on his decision and injecting the first tremor of high excitement in his life. He had miscalculated their use of him. He had hoped for something more flamboyant than the covert, almost clerical, nature of his assignments, material lists from companies he financed, descriptions of projects still on drawing boards.

But there at first he had the high, intense excitement of Ginny, whose elegance was as natural as her revolutionary fervor was assumed. There was an old saw that said a liberal could be made a conservative by one mugging. In Ginny's case it only took a white wedding gown and a few bars of Purcell to change a revolutionary into a Junior Leaguer.

The next time he had a chance to look up he was a bank president (thanks to Ginny's father's early demise), a husband, father, and pillar of the community. And bored to death except for those rare assignments that came through. Skiing had been a challenge for a while and a whirl at aerobatic flying. The P-39 had held its kicks and some of the women, Eloise in particular, had kept him half off balance enough to be worth the time. But the Flying Mick was going to be the big one, the springboard that would catapult him into Vladimir's full attention. Then he would have jobs to do worth something. Then he would come into his own.

He frowned at even that passing thought of Eloise. The little bitch, breaking up was no big deal, but her and her cards had set a pall on his head. Gretchen always goaded him for being superstitious; it was a big tease with her. He wasn't superstitious in the way Russians are supposed to be, but no man likes to be told even by a half-baked hippie girl that he was marked for death.

She had picked him up at a bar with a new line.

"I read in the cards that you wanted to buy me a drink."

He had laughed and turned only to find the laughter tightened to a whistle. She was different looking in the best kind of way, a face as cool as water running free and a body that didn't stop. She was clearly a year or two short of the twenty-one she claimed, but her face held enough maturity that the bartender handed over her drink.

She had shown him the tarot cards right away. "They run my life," she said matter-of-factly. "It smooths things out."

And it had been smooth between them from the first. She called all the shots, or the cards did. She asked nothing more from him than their violent matings, first in her walk-up pad and later in the apartment he insisted on renting for her.

Everything about her, the tawny abundance of her hair, her lean, boyish body, even the ragged brilliance of her clothing, turned him on.

He should have known it would end as it had begun, pointlessly except for that damned parting shot of hers that he couldn't get out of his head.

Between Ginny and the kids, the day before Easter was crowded. He had told her he would be there at two but it was four-thirty when he eased his car into the marked slot in the alley behind her place. All the slots were special, the Shoe Palace, Angie's Flowers To Go, and the numbered slots for the flats. He could leave the car there all night when he had the chance to stay.

A slit-eyed tomcat was sleeping on the porch when he reached the top of the stairs. It stared at him and rumbled rhythmically with welcome.

She had opened the door at about the tenth ring. She hadn't bothered to dress. A thin shirt hung from her shoulders, revealing the inner curves of her breasts above that firm belly. She was yawning as he barked at her.

"For Christ's sake, cover yourself up," he had said, his mind on the busy alley at his back.

She had shrugged and stepped backward. The table was piled with folded papers topped by a soiled mug with a spoon sticking from the top. The room stank of wine and sleep. Jeans and a plaid shirt lay abandoned between them and the unmade bed. He reached for her, feeling for her mouth as she backed away.

She shook her head, bracing her hand against his shoulder. "You're late," she said firmly.

"So I'm sorry as all hell," he admitted. "I did my level best." Her naked back against his hand was all it had taken to rouse him.

"I was ready," she explained quietly like she was a soft-boiled egg or something. "I was ready then and I'm not now."

"Oh come on," he teased, grinning at her. Sometimes she liked a little combat just for variety. Gripping her body with one arm he slid the other hand between her thighs, groping.

The curse was involuntary as the slime of semen covered his wrist.

Her eyes stayed the same, level and disinterested. Her mouth didn't even reveal apprehension.

"I told you," she repeated. "I was ready and you weren't here."

He looked about as if the guy was stupid enough to still be there. He glanced around to realize she wasn't even watching him. Instead, she had pulled the cards from the table and sat down with them on the bed, leaning over so that her long hair brushed the tender inside of her thighs.

"What in hell are you doing?" he challenged her.

"I want to show you this," she said, concentrating on setting out the cards.

Her voice was strange. The vitality was gone from it, the ordinary rich variety of tone. She was on something. That was it, she was on something. He grasped the thought with relief, sitting on the bed beside her.

"Come on, honey," he coaxed. "What did you take? What are you on?"

She was undeniably different. Even with his face that near, her expression was withdrawn as if she saw him from a great distance. She stirred away from him and caught that mass of hair and twisted it behind her back. She looked about Gretchen's age when she did that, softly rounded of face and virginal.

"Now watch what comes up and you'll know you're through."

He chuckled, sliding a hand under her rump. "So I'm mad as hell that you're such an alley cat but we're not through."

"I didn't say that," she reminded him. "You're through. I've seen it coming and now it's really close. Look at that, there are only death cards for you anymore."

He stared at the skulls marching across the rumpled coverlet. Only then did it register on him what she was saying.

He rose, laughing in spite of himself. "What a half-baked kid you are, Ellie. You and your cards."

But she had always been that way, he remembered. She had picked him up that way and held him by the same token, calling him on that unlisted line at the bank, telling him that the cards had said he needed her. By God, they had always been right.

"So now your cards have turned against me?" he laughed.

She wouldn't soften up for anything. Her face stayed sober and serene. "I was ready and you didn't come," she said like a recitation. "I was going to give it to you for the last time and now it's too late. Maybe there's sex after death?" she added, smiling a little at her corniness.

He stared at her a long moment. He wished he could be mad enough to hit her or care enough to. It just wasn't there. He had had a good thing with her and would miss it. But there was this funny thing about women. Sooner or later they open a window into their heads and that extra glimpse shows a landscape with no mystery. She was a beautifully shaped kid with an ingenious approach to screwing, but she was still half-cocked. That he could live without. The thing he didn't like was this talk of death, that line of skulls.

He pulled a couple of bills from his pocket and tossed them on the row of cards.

"Next's month's rent," he told her. "Happy landing if you ever get off of what bugs you."

In the car he realized the semen was still on his hands, crusting as it dried. He spat on it and wiped furiously, but it burned a little on his flesh. Once out of the alley he threw the handkerchief out the window. He left the car in the bank pool parking area, grateful he had never slipped up and used his own. The discontinuance of the telephone line was the matter of a memo on Monday morning.

The death's-head thing made him edgy all through the meal that Ginny and Aunt Iris had held for him. He drank more than he needed and Ginny looked at him puzzled.

"Something the matter, Stan?"

He shook his head and grinned. "Nothing that can't be fixed with a Phillips screwdriver."

She had giggled and her Aunt Iris looked confused. It was an old joke between them from the faulty refrigerator door in their first apartment.

He didn't realize the phone was ringing until Gretchen called him. "Somebody named Rick," she said. "From the dusting place."

He groaned and laid his napkin down.

Ginny leaned back so that her hair brushed his arm as he passed her. "If you need a Phillips for that, just whistle," she teased.

When he had come into the company they had expanded the Flying Mick, which meant more pilots as well as planes. The only man of Dobbs's own choice was this Rick who, for all that he was an excellent pilot, was also a crybaby. Knowing where his job had come from, it was always Dobbs that he cried to.

Dobbs listened to him complain that Mac had singled him out to pick on. He recited the litany—overloaded planes, schedules too tight, hours too long.

Dobbs listened, finally promising him he'd call Mac and talk to him.

"Not tonight I hope," Ginny said from the door. "We promised the Farrows."

"Not tonight," he agreed. "Early tomorrow. Very early," he added, grinning at her.

She chuckled a little. "I hope he's an early riser, for his own sake," she said, knowing that Stan would be awake and up before the first birds stirred in the eucalyptus beyond the pool.

Booze being no friend to Stan's pillow, he was awake and into his study even earlier than usual. Eloise's damned cards were no help either; just the thought of them hung in his mind.

He had promised Rick and he had to call, to keep the kid's confidence. But he mustn't let Maguire get to him the way he usually did. The Flying Mick was his ticket to a faster track only if he could play it right. The idea had been only a germ when he first met Heinemann. By the time Walter came back asking for a loan, it was a full-fledged plan. With a legal flying service under your control there was no limit to air reconnaissance possibilities. Half the damned bay area was plastered with military installations. Critical shipping moved in and out of the Gate with the tide. Who would pay any attention to World War II Stearmans cruising that area? Who would figure on their being equipped with the state-of-the-art in telescopic cameras?

But first he had to shake Mac out of his spot and put in a manager he could control. He even had the man, Jackson, waiting in the wings and getting restive.

What was the best way to play Mac? There was no possibility of friendship between them, that had been clear from day one.

The strip had been a madhouse. Nobody greeted him and Walter. Nobody even looked up. A couple of guys in dirty jumpsuits were loading hopper trucks while a Chicano gassed a Stearman poised on the apron with its motor running. A telephone rang steadily in the trailer that served as an office, as the Stearman lifted and another one came in.

"Where's Mac?" Heinemann had shouted. The kid waved to the hangar behind him. Mac came up from under the plane's hood, blinking. After glancing at his oily hands, he nodded to them.

"Good to meet you," he said, his eyes studious on Stan.

"Something wrong with this baby?" Heinemann asked.

"Handles funny," Mac replied. The plane's pilot, over by the hangar, nodded at the introduction.

Mac didn't so much dismiss them as just not credit their presence with any importance.

"Go get some coffee," he ordered. "I'll be right with you."

Instead of getting coffee, they watched Mac take the plane up. With patient perfection he put the Stearman through its measured paces, one after another. Exhibitionist, Dobbs thought, damned Irish exhibitionist. Grudgingly he registered that nobody could have improved on the timing of that slow aileron roll, the carefully angled caravelle.

When Mac set her down he shouted at the mechanic, "Pull her out of traffic and dig out her tail. That's where the problem is."

Only then did he join them.

"Dobbs," he repeated, frowning. "Sounds English, but you don't look it."

"I changed it," Dobbs said. "It was too tough to spell."

"Polack," Mac said like a judgment.

The flush came on Stan's face without his will. The damned Irish. They were all cut from the same piece of flat shit. He'd had some rough time from the bastards as a kid and later in the service. The Irishman is always the one with the stick.

"Where you from?" Mac asked, still eyeing him.

"Ohio," Dobbs had replied, forcing the man's eyes with his own. Laying it there against Mac, the Italian silk suit, the gold watch, the banker's tailoring. "How about you?"

"Pennsylvania," Mac grunted, a wry grin plucking at the corners of his mouth. Right then the lines were drawn. The old days again, laboring Irish against Polack miners. Never mind that Stanley's blood was undiluted Ukrainian. They were all Polacks to the Irish and the Irish carried the sticks.

The mechanic had brought an apologetic grin back to them. "Compacted dust," he admitted. "Bunched up back there in the tail section. Four or five pounds."

Mac grunted. "That's enough."

Soon after that, Stan had made his first effort to dislodge Mac. "This is a bigger operation now than Mac has any experience with," he pointed out to Heinemann. "Let's bring on a new chief pilot to manage the place."

Walter had stared as if amazed. "You can't be serious. This is a business built on that man. And don't worry, he'll run it just like it was all still his own."

He made himself seven promises about keeping cool when he called Mac. He broke all of them and had to end up telling Walter Heinemann what had happened before Mac got his ear.

"I'll get him," he promised the empty room. "He hasn't got a pig's idea of what he's up against with me."

Gretchen's tap was startling on his door. "Quit talking to yourself and come to breakfast," she ordered with the laughter just behind her voice.

"Okay, honey," he called. "Be right there."

While he had brooded, the terrace had blossomed with silver and china and a long-legged champagne cooler. Gretchen had exchanged her Speed-o suit for a sundress. Ginny was waving, smiling.

As always, Ginny's eggs Benedict were fantastic. The ham melted under his fork and the egg burst in a golden volcano through the tartness of hollandaise. Even Lafe closed his book to eat.

Gretchen looked up at him, a thin stream of pool water still working its way down from her dripping scalp.

"What were you chattering to yourself about when I came to call you?"

"A problem," Stan told her. "Just a problem."

"Not at the bank," Ginger protested.

He shook his head.

"Dad's other life," Gretchen laughed. "The spacy Irish or whatever."

One of those wordless dialogues passed between Ginger and Lafe. The boy's dark eyes silently searched his mother's face.

"The crop-dusting company," she explained. "The Flying Mick."

Lafe raised his eyebrows critically at his sister and went back to his book.

The shadow from the open work of the lawn chair was an irregular pattern of dark against the pale of the terrace tile. For God's sake, for one horrifying moment it looked like that row of death skulls laid out on Eloise's bed.

He reached for the champagne bottle to refill first Ginger's glass and then his own.

5

Mac Maguire

Blakeslea, California, Easter, April 14

Mac watched Rick taxi the plane down the line. Sweat followed the canals of his face as he stared against the sun. The weathered Stearman dragged its beer belly down the runway. Damned few feet of macadam were left when she cleared the ground. At about fifty feet Rick swung her around and pointed her heavy nose east toward the job.

Mac's anger tempered to grudging amusement. Son of a bitch, if that Rick hadn't given him the finger from the cockpit as the plane passed him. Just like Toby. Cocky little bastards, the lot of them. Kids like that were so damned quick on the reflex that it almost, not quite but almost, made up for their lack of judgment . . . and manners.

"Lousy little punk," he murmured, chuckling to himself.

"You might say," Evert agreed drily. The mechanic, squinting at the light and wiping his hands, stepped from the shop to watch the takeoff.

Mac grunted.

"But that one has always known how to get to you," Evert reminded him.

That was true enough. Rick had come when Dobbs bought in. Was it because he had been hired on Dobbs's say-so that Mac found him hard to stomach? He had a slithery way of not meeting Mac's eyes that got on his nerves.

"But anybody can get to me by shutting down his motor during a refill," Mac pointed out. Any pilot who ever tried to prop a hot Stearman knew how much time he would lose with that trick.

"He'll be wishing he had that flying time back come sundown," Evert predicted.

As Evert disappeared into the shop, Mac stared at the spot of sky where Rick's plane had been. There had been more words between himself and Rick than Evert knew. Even knowing how prickly Rick was about advice, Mac had warned him about this job.

"That's a mean little field over there at Lucky," he had cautioned. "Watch out for that stand of live oak when the wind rises."

"I've worked the field before," Rick reminded him sullenly, fastening his helmet without meeting Mac's eyes.

"Just take it easy," Mac insisted, a little sharply. "We ain't got buggies to burn, you know."

With calculated insolence, Rick had turned to stare at the spare parts of old Stearmans heaped by the hangar. Mac cursed silently as Rick gunned the plane off. Rick was cocky, no two ways about it. Mac was also damned sure he was the whiner who had been mewling to Dobbs about pilot overwork.

"Dusting's a man's job," he muttered crossly. He was still staring after the plane when the pain hit. He winced and flipped the butt of his cigarette away. Thinking better of it, he ground it out with the heel of his boot. He stared at his injured finger with disbelief. God, wouldn't that little rotter like to know that he had stood there like a reuben at a skin show until he burnt his newly tender finger on that damned fag? He touched his tongue to the whitened flesh and turned back to the office.

That sweet poison smell filled his head again the minute the cigarette was gone. He stopped to light another, cupping his hand around the match that struggled against the breeze circling the hangar. Maybe someday he would be able to watch a takeoff without wondering how the bastard would come down. You'd think that someday a man could get on top of his gut-dread of death.

During the war a friend's death was an eraser across a flight schedule board. The dusting business was its own war, take away the flags and the C-rations. It was men against ground currents, against their own cockiness, against the stubborn pride that kept a man's hand frozen on the stick when he was blind with fatigue. And wires. Always the wires.

Toby. The etching of wires against an endless Texas sky. That lunge of pain in his chest shallowed his breath. He forced his mind to the stack of parts Rick had goaded him with.

"Old Stearmans never die," his first dusting boss had told him. "They just get reshuffled again and dealt out like marked aces."

But there's no trip back for a son. Meg's voice, hesitant across the miles. "Jug-eared like his father."

In Texas Mac had seen the plane Toby died in. Now all the wrecked Stearmans seemed to flower with brown stains on their dashboards where Toby had bled, shining tool marks where his body had been cut out.

He shook his head crossly. A man who looks back will sure as hell stumble on what's coming. It was Dobbs he had to worry about. If he could only figure out what the man was after. Talk about a cold war. You knew trouble was coming but never where or when it would bring you up short. Waiting wore a man to his marrow.

Thank God there was enough to do to distract him, the shop

to run, schedules to meet, the ranchers to be stroked down. And Walter Heinemann was behind him when Dobbs got out of hand. The telephone's muted jangle came from inside the larger trailer. He turned to the sound.

While the smaller trailer was his home, this larger one was the world of his days. It held not only his office and Cramar's cubicle, but a rough pilot lounge where the men could rest out of the sun while they ate or waited on planes. There was always coffee if one wanted to dignify Cramar's brew with that name.

Three signs decorated the panel beside the door. The largest identified these quarters as "The Flying Mick, James P. Maguire, Manager." On a square of cardboard beneath that, ruder letters read "Stork Club, West," followed by the legend "On these chairs rest the dumbest bastards left alive." Mac liked the bottom notice best. Handwritten on frail paper that fluttered in the wind, it simply identified the inner space as "Cramar's Cranny." While Mac would be hard pressed to define the word *cranny*, it suggested the dark retreat of a spider that was somehow suitable for his bookkeeper, paymaster and general harridan of all office work.

Thelma Cramar herself was somewhat spidery, as lean as grass and dry as the valley dust. Her dark eyes sparkled the vitriol her tongue didn't dare release around those guys. She rode the phone and shuffled endless insurance papers and government forms and brewed coffee that would float an egg. She also wept in a cramped, convulsive, heaving way when one of "the men" got hurt. Or hit the wires.

Both trailers had once been blue but the constant wind-blown chemicals had tainted their color. The windows were clouded and through the open door a double trail of ants passed Mac civilly, coming and going from the wastebasket.

Cramar occasionally made war on these foraging columns with spray can and broom. Mac himself figured that any crawling thing surviving in this death factory deserved the mangled garbage it could glean from discarded lunch scraps.

Mac's own desk was arranged for utility. At Evert's mild complaint that it was so dirty it gave him sties to look at it, Mac snorted.

"If you are into shiny desks, go ogle the ones we taxpayers have bought down at the courthouse. There's work done here."

Among the stacks of papers and clipboards was an ashtray surrounded by near misses and Mac's mug, villainous with dregs. He had bought his coat stand for its resemblance to an army captain he had served under. Its great knob head was solid pine and its wide but skinny shoulders caught his jacket from any angle. The keyboard above his desk held keys he could not have identified for his life. The only one that mattered was the one with the yellow tag and this one he would not let stray for the same price.

By nature Mac was a man to rebel against rules. The regulations on storage and maintenance of the chemicals of his trade were the only exception to this. The premises were cluttered with warning notices listing the toxic chemicals in the order of their deadliness. Some got a man orally, some through the skin and others just by inhalation. Some red-flag names appeared on all lists—Tepp, Thimet, Parathion, Endrin—the lists went on and on.

From the time those chemicals were delivered until the containers that couldn't be cleaned out were picked up on Saturday evening, Mac felt the weight of them. The key marked yellow for contamination was a part of that weight. Only that key opened the gates to the fenced enclosure in the hangar where the poisons were stored. Mac wanted to be able to see that key every time he lifted his eyes.

Cramar's back stiffened as he slammed the schedule board on his desk.

"The boss called," she told him. "He's on the way out."

Mac froze, his gut suddenly tightening. Dobbs wouldn't dare. Not after that last call of his. He wouldn't dare come say right out what he had said on the phone.

"Mr. Hineyman," Cramar explained, "called while you were out there with Rick. Should be along any time."

"Didn't say what he wanted, did he?"

When she shook her head the strings that secured her glasses swayed like spider webs. So Dobbs had dragged Heinemann into their fight.

Let him. Let him bleat to Heinemann all he damn pleased. Heinemann knew where the company's bread was buttered. He knew Mac didn't push pilots for the fun of it but because of time. That Rick was running behind schedule wasn't entirely the man's fault. All the trucks had been in distant fields, supplying other planes. With the Lucky Frank field only ten miles away, it saved time to bring in the plane. But the kid had to speed it up. Mac had promised Len Frank to be through and off his fields by Monday. It would be a helluva lot easier if Frank had taken out that clump of live oak. Mac had flown that field enough to know how tricky it was to pull out of it with any air moving. Rick had to keep his head on it. Any pilot worth his bread could handle that lift.

With a freshly lit Camel in his hand to smother the chemical stench, he turned to the schedule just as the German shepherds exploded into warning behind their fence. Mac rose to see Walter Heinemann's Porsche ease to a stop outside.

"You might throw out that acid and brew some coffee," he told Cramar, starting out. "Just in case."

With Heinemann himself he barely exchanged greetings before challenging. "You here on business or pleasure?"

"A little of both," Walter replied, peering at the windsock. "What do you say?"

"Five to seven miles an hour," Mac gauged. "It'll build up later. Going to take the Mick up?" Mac wished he would. Maybe seeing Heinemann cutting those wide pieces of the spring sky would jog his butt into the driver's seat again.

Heinemann shook his head. "Can you get away to have lunch?"

Mac paused. A motor whined from Evert's shop. The boys were readying for Rick's return from Lucky Frank. "Just for a little," he decided. "I ain't fancy."

Heinemann grinned and slid into his car. "I wasn't thinking of the Cliff House."

The valley looked different from the seat of the sports car. The canals mirrored an indecently blue sky and masses of wild morning glories flowed along the roadside.

Mary's Steakhouse was just outside the city limits. You could smell it a half mile off, a mingled scent of beer and broiling beef. The bar always hummed and Mary, God knows how, kept a crew of fresh-faced country girls who waited on tables with easy amiability.

Heinemann cradled a beer as he studied the menu.

"Not fancy," Mac said. "But the beef's hot and the beer cold."

Heinemann grinned, handing the menu back. "New York strip with Roquefort and baked," he told the waiting girl.

"This has to be the pleasure part," Mac said when he had echoed the order for himself. "What's on your mind?"

Heinemann stirred uneasily. "I won't horse around, Mac. Dobbs got me out of bed with some tale of a fight between you two."

"He called me," Mac was defensive. "Since that last blowup I have been a saint on loading so he finds something new to bitch about."

"You're caught in the middle, aren't you?" Heinemann mused. "Between Dobbs and your ranchers."

Mac nodded. "For my money the ranchers come first. We're not in the business of coddling pilots."

Heinemann pushed over the bottled sauce like a peace offering.

"Dobbs thinks you're coming down too hard, running schedules too tight." His voice trailed off. "Pilots are superstitious, you know."

"So how does that apply?" Mac challenged.

Heinemann raised his eyes to Mac's. The sudden blue startled Mac's own eyes down. "Come on, Mac," Heinemann said quietly.

"Toby didn't die here," Mac argued. "Not out of our shop."

"They felt it that close. Dobbs says they feel you are trying to get back at them for still being alive."

"What a bunch of crap," Mac exploded, pushing his plate away. "We've got a job to do here. We've made promises. We're shorthanded. The rains stayed late . . ."

Heinemann shrugged. "The truth is not material, Mac. But neither of us can do our jobs with Dobbs raising hell like this."

Mac sighed. "What can I do? You know pilots, especially young guys like ours. Let up on them even a little and they get slipshod. Then you really have the devil to pay."

"We're partners, Mac. We've been partners too long to fight over what can't be solved. We're stuck with Dobbs so we have to figure out how to handle him."

"If I could only figure out why he's so dead set on driving me out," Mac said. "I just can't read the guy and still he keeps pressing."

"He puzzles me too," Heinemann admitted. "Maybe he just hassles because it's his style. As for you, it was your shop first and it won't run any other way. But we're stuck with him. We made the plunge, new planes, more staff, the new runway. We can't make it without his capital. Ease up a little. Don't push so hard. Give the pilots a chance to get over their weegies."

"I wish to hell they'd have their weegies in the off-season," Mac grunted.

"All of us have things we wish we could handle better than we do," Heinemann reminded him quietly.

Mac emptied his beer in silence. He felt the chill of the mug against his tender palm. All of us have things we can't handle.

On the way back to the strip Mac realized that his belly wasn't boiling for a change. Talking things over like that had made things look a little easier. He straightened in his seat. Hell, this hassle with Dobbs was something he could handle. With Heinemann behind him he could handle it no sweat.

Before the car stopped, Thelma Cramar was hailing them from the trailer steps. She was white around the mouth and her words tumbled.

"They radioed in from Lucky Frank," she told Mac. "They need help. Rick didn't clear the trees on his last run."

"How is he?" Heinemann asked in a tone cold enough to give a man a spine chill.

"It was him on the radio with Evert saying he needed the plane hauled in."

Heinemann's face seemed suddenly closed but his hand was quick to Mac's in a firm handshake.

"I'll clear out, Mac. You've obviously got some moving to do."

Mac nodded his thanks. "I am sure as hell sorry," he said. "I'll think about what you said."

"Please do," Heinemann urged, kicking the motor to life and smiling that careful way. "Please do."

6

Tuesday, April 18

The rice season generated a mysterious power of its own, assuming control of the Flying Mick for its own ruthless fulfillment. Men who were jocular in other seasons became morose and irritable bastards. The camaraderie of the pilot's lounge degenerated to grunts and silence. Fortunately the slander fell on minds too dulled by fatigue to absorb the enormity of the insults they were subjected to.

Hours lost their credibility, displaced by the critical importance of minutes. A fourteen-hour day became a shattered eternity of takeoffs and landings. You couldn't pay any attention to wind. You simply took off from short, slippery strips damned glad they were even twenty-five feet wide. You fought everything, ditches, canal banks, standpipes and fences. Every eight minutes you set down or took off, either whipping empty or sluggish from a maximum weight load. Even the plane had its teeth out for you on grounds of abuse.

The food was brown-bagged or greasy and chilled. You gulped it in haste for heartburn at leisure. Only the cargo changed, from fertilizer to seed and then to top dressing with a momentum that promised to sustain itself forever, dropping men off without looking back.

At least the rice season played no favorites. They were all in it to their eyeballs. The pilots who hit the field at dawn liked to ride Evert about lolling around his house half the day. It was true enough. By midday he arrived to cope with the complaints mounting on his shop blackboard. From that moment he juggled one crisis after another until his and Mac's were the only lights south of town for a hundred miles.

When Mac saw Rick's plane downed at Lucky Frank's he fought himself hard for control. Rick had no damned business setting it down there when he could as easily have flown it in for repairs and saved the full day it would take to haul it in. With Heinemann's words still fresh in his mind he swallowed his fury and got Evert in by nine that next morning with an extra mechanic to speed up the repair. With the best of luck the duster would be out of service for an entire week.

Mac watched the flurry in the shop glumly. He was convinced that if the sullen bastard hadn't gone out there on the prod he would never have snagged those oaks. Now Rick, without a scratch on him, was staying in town as Mac shuffled schedules to move the jobs faster. Any pilot worth his salt works alongside the mechanic when his plane is out. If it wasn't the middle of rice season and himself already shorthanded, he would have fired the punk for that alone. Still he wondered how much of his resentment came from the smell of Dobbs about the man.

Everything that could go wrong did that week. A radioed summons for a prop repair took both Mac and Evert from the shop to a field twenty-five miles away. The pilot had blinked too close to a mess of wires. By the time he saw them there wasn't any over or under left. He had done the only possible thing to save himself and the plane. He aimed straight at the wires and took them on his nose. The spinning mass looked like Christmas tinsel before they started cutting the wires out.

When the wind shifted on Thursday, a pilot was seeding with an inexperienced flagman. The pilot signaled the flagman by flying low and pointing to the other side of the field. The flagman moved all right but failed to leave a marker. By the time the pilot realized he was seeding the same stretch a second time, they had double-seeded half a field. At the price of the rice seed the rancher had a right to raise all the hell he did.

Mac was still shuffling his Friday afternoon paper when Cramar rang his line.

"Dobbs," she said quietly.

With half a Camel pluming from the ashtray, Mac lit another, inhaled deeply and took the call.

"Maguire here," he said carefully.

"Stanley Dobbs. What's this about the kid being hospitalized from poison over there?"

"News to me," Mac said. "Where did you hear that?" The heaviness of undigested burrito stirred in his belly.

"I have my sources," Dobbs told him. "How liable are we if he dies?"

"The whole thing is news to me," Mac repeated. "Was it our poison or are you just guessing? We handle that stuff like it was dynamite, run all the technical checks. When did this happen? Where? Do you have a name?"

"Donnie Sutter," Dobbs replied. "Five years old, admitted to Blakeslea Memorial Hospital sometime last night."

"I'll look into it," Mac told him. "We aren't the only sprayers working this valley, you know. And there isn't a line on those check sheets that we don't observe to the letter."

"Sure, Mac," Dobbs said, his tone heavy with sarcasm.

Mac wheeled on Cramar. "Got any contacts at the hospital? Never mind. Call Jake Loman and tell him I need to speak to him quick."

"Can I tell him what about?" Cramar asked.

"We pay his legal fees without question, he takes my calls the same way."

He turned back to his desk, but it didn't work. Five years old. He remembered Toby at five. His body had been too long for his legs at that age, giving him a curiously dwarfish look. Still a lot of baby fat on him, but his teeth already starting to fall out.

It had been ten days since Meg's call. He tried to remember the girl Kathy Potter but couldn't put the name with a face. She had only been one of the crowd that battered through the house in Toby's wake. She was a woman now, old enough to follow Toby to Texas and get knocked up. Woman enough to bear a child but not enough to keep it.

It was a lot of damned foolishness for Meg even to think of taking the kid. How could she support a kid by herself like that? The least she could do is let him off the hook, tell him what had happened. Instead there had been the click of that phone and the dial tone droning in his ear.

It was dark when the attorney returned his call.

"Court ran late," Loman explained. "What's up?"

"Nothing I hope," Mac told him. "Got a call from my partner about a kid being poisoned out here. Something about poisoned fruit."

"You been spraying fruit?" Loman asked.

"Only rice," Mac told him. "We did some dormant peach spraying back in March but it was copper oleate, which is exempt from restrictions because it's not that toxic. The ground was too wet for the growers to get their own rigs in. But that doesn't rule out somebody having a pest infestation and using something stronger."

"Got the family name, any details?" Loman asked.

"Donnie Sutter." Then compulsively, "Five years old."

"Christ," Loman groaned. "I'll get back to you."

The schedules were finished by eleven. He was throwing the yellow copies on Cramar's desk when Loman called back.

"Your partner was right. The kid got sick and was already in tough shape before his folks bothered to get him into emergency."

"And he got it off of fruit?" Mac asked.

"He apparently picked a lot of it, stuffing his shirt and jeans pockets with freshly sprayed green fruit. It is too hard to bite. Is that stuff you use toxic on contact?"

"Twenty of them are," Mac told him. "How in hell did he get hold of all that green fruit?"

"His folks have a trailer parked beside the Robbins's spread. He must have gone over the fence for it, or under, who knows?"

Guilty relief flowed through him. "Robbins isn't one of our accounts. Lamar Flying Service does his work. But I know Robbins. He would have had the place posted if he sprayed fruit. It's the law and he's that kind of guy. I bet it was posted in Spanish and Chinese as well as English."

"Five-year-olds don't read much," Loman reminded him. "In any case I am glad the Flying Mick isn't involved."

"Hell, we're all involved," Mac pointed out. "There's always a rabble ready to jump on crop-dusters. You'd think we were the enemies of the world. They can't seem to grasp how much easier it is to starve people to death than it is to keep them in food."

"Easy, easy, Mac," Loman urged. "The nurse told me if the kid held out through the weekend he might live."

Mac lay sleepless in the dark of his trailer bunk. The muscles in his bad leg jumped sporadically trying to get themselves untwisted for the night. Why did he keep seeing Donnie Sutter as a jug-eared kid with freckles, all strapped with tubes and bottles? He'd never even seen the kid.

And Dobbs. Dobbs kept weaving into his head. Jake Loman lived two blocks off the square and his office was right on it. He was in and out of the courthouse, which was a goddamned magnet for all the gossip in the area. Yet Jake Loman had to check into the story about a poisoned kid that Dobbs had called about from Atherton.

As Mac shifted onto his side, a prickling shiver ran up his spine. His mother, Katie Maguire, had said that feeling was a goose walking on a man's grave. She was a superstitious old woman, God rest her soul. But there was danger and he was caught in the middle of it and he didn't even know what it was all about. Dobbs was in it and his local spy, whoever that was. From somewhere in the fens of his Irish soul a wraith had risen to waver in his mind like an omen. Toby was gone and Meg was off on some crazy trip with a bastard kid. All he had was the Flying Mick. And his freedom. At least his freedom.

Ginger Dobbs leaned to kiss Stan's forehead when the evening news was over. "I'll go warm the bed," she told him. "See you when your call comes in."

Stan Dobbs trailed his hand down her arm to loose at her fingers. "It can't be long," he assured her. Her smile stayed in his mind. God he was lucky in that woman. And other things. All at once the cards had begun to fall his way. He saw Eloise, the strands of hair loose beside her absorbed face as she studied the tarot cards. He was shaking his head as the phone chimed across the room.

"What did your partner say about the kid?" Jackson asked.

"It caught him cold," Dobbs replied. "He hadn't heard a word."

"He could have been lying," Jackson suggested.

"Not this time," Dobbs assured him. "He was caught flat-footed."

Jackson chuckled. "It was pure luck that I heard the story before the paper came out. It'll be all over by tomorrow. Did your shop spread that poison?"

"That isn't important. The Flying Mick is insured against everything but the Second Coming. I got what I wanted. Mac knows he's being watched. He knows he better keep on his toes."

Jackson grunted satisfaction. "Are you still thinking of going down to check out that Citabria in San Jose? The price looks good."

"Sure thing," Dobbs agreed. "We'll give it a look anyway."

"Sunday okay?" Jackson asked. "I could be down there early."

"Sunday it is," Dobbs circled his calendar. "In the meantime keep in touch. I like being a step ahead."

"My pleasure," Jackson replied.

Dobbs sat a moment staring at the phone. Thank God he had chanced onto Jackson. Or had it been the other way around?

Mac had to go. Replacing him would have been the first hurdle with Heinemann when he finally saw the light. Jackson solved that. Heinemann would be as impressed with the Texan as Dobbs had been that first day Jackson contacted him at the bank.

"He hasn't a card," his secretary had apologized, "but he insists on seeing you. His name is Jackson, Tex Jackson."

"That's it?" he asked.

She grinned. "He said he has twenty years at dusting and is the best damned pilot in the game."

"Modest." Dobbs had grinned back. "How old?"

She frowned thoughtfully. "Forty maybe. A big man and lean."

Jackson had come on strong. Undismayed by the opulence of a bank president's office, he had crossed swiftly to Dobbs's hand. His one-sided smile produced a crease like an old dimple gone to pot. His eyes were ice blue returning Dobbs's gaze.

"So you are the best damned pilot in the game?" Dobbs asked, waving him to a chair.

Jackson nodded, tugging at skintight jeans to give himself knee room.

"How many hours?"

Jackson laughed. "Hours, hell. Any stick jockey can keep a score card. Ask me how many landings and takeoffs a man can do in fifteen years of twelve-hour days."

"You got that number?" Dobbs laughed.

Jackson shrugged. "Texas and Louisiana. All rice."

"How come the best duster in the country is looking for work at the peak of the season?" Dobbs challenged.

"The same reason I haven't brought a reference from the last shop," Jackson replied. "I fell out with the boss and walked off."

"What was your beef?" Dobbs asked, preparing himself for the traditional whines of overloading, overwork, and little pay. Jackson came back from another slant.

"Political."

"Political," Dobbs repeated. "Now come on."

"The rednecked bastard was shoving it to his ground crew like hot lead. A genuine unreconstructed rebel. What you can't live with stomp out or stamp out." Jackson's eyes challenged Dobbs.

"What if I don't have a job for you?"

"I'll wait," Jackson said easily. "I can smell trouble in your shop a mile off." He lifted his shoulders again. "Trouble means change. I'll just stay handy."

"I'm supposed to take all this on your word."

"Hell, no," Jackson said. "I'll fan out my licenses and you lend me a plane. If ten minutes in the air doesn't sell you, then I shove on."

"That's fair enough," Dobbs agreed. "But there's no job open."

"Not yet," Jackson reminded him.

In the two weeks since that meeting, he had seen a lot of the man. He was a good listener and knew flying. His open amazement when Dobbs told him about the P-39 was pretty satisfying. Maybe Dobbs had told him more about the Flying Mick than he meant to, but maybe not. It was only a matter of time until Mac was out and Jackson would get the berth. Dobbs would see to that. In the meantime, Tex had been obliging.

He had gone back to the valley to wait around.

"Get to know the guys. Keep your ears open. Make friends,"

Dobbs had suggested. "I'll pick up your expenses and some pocket change."

"Straight out or loan?" Jackson asked.

"Straight out," Dobbs replied. Fifty dollars a day wasn't going to make Tex or break himself. It was already beginning to bring interest with Jackson's good nose for news.

Dobbs rose and flipped out the lights. It was silent upstairs. Ginger would be sleeping with a book still open on her chest.

As he had told Jackson, this would help keep Mac on his toes. It was a good position to start running from.

7

Sausalito, California, April 19

Pat September looked up as her employer, Walter Heinemann, entered the office. Her tentative smile implied that she was in awe of him.

Once she opened her mouth, it was clear she was not. Walter still liked that smile as a teasing suggestion of the girl that his secretary might have been, given another time and a different metabolism.

She was a small girl whose dark hair looped above an apple-shaped forehead. With her knit clinging to the curve of her hips and her remarkable breasts she appeared to be exactly what she was not—a soft yielding girl only half inclined to turn into woman.

In truth Pat September was militant in a struggle that Walter privately dignified with capital letters, THE PRIVATE WAR OF PAT SEPTEMBER. Pat's zealous dedication involved no slogans or organizations. This was a vicious private combat, an unremitting civil war against her own healthy flesh.

She pulled a letter from her machine as she met his eyes.

"You're back early." It was more commendation than reproach. "Stanley Dobbs called twice, wants you to return his call after two. Mrs. Prescott has decided to go ahead with the yawl and when will you have it ready for them to sail?"

"In the same breath, I suppose." Walter laughed.

Pat's eyebrows expressed an opinion of Mrs. Prescott before she frowned intently at her typewriter.

"Something else?" Heinemann prodded. "Crane maybe?"

"Crane," she repeated with relief. "He is at Corinthian. Be back late afternoon. Oh yes. And I lost two pounds."

"Congratulations." He turned away to conceal his smile. "Just don't melt all the way away before payday."

"Fat chance," she replied, then groaned. "I retract that term."

With coat off and tie loosened, Walter settled to his desk. The staccato of Pat's typing was soothing. "Two pounds," she had said. He had not varied more than that much in the past thirty years. But Pat! By his shirtsleeve guess she had lost two hundred pounds during the three years she had worked for him. On a size-ten female that represented one full recycling and a healthy start on a second. All this without looking a shade different as she stormed into the office at nine and raced the clock out at five.

His calendar showed that he had stolen seven minutes from the world this morning. Two appointments had gone off like clockwork, leaving him forty-five minutes before his lunch date with his attorney at twelve-thirty.

The view from his window caught the angle of the bay. The sea fog that usually cleared by ten still dragged sullenly across the headlands. It stood mast high on the sailboats nudging each other in the marina. But across the bay a thin blue line revealed the valley bathed in its usual blazing sun. The Flying Mick should be running on schedule today.

"Dobbs, after 2:00 P.M." He made the calendar entry with a grimace, and hoped Dobbs had nothing on his mind. After Rick's accident on Easter day, he and Mac had agreed that Mac would communicate with Dobbs only through Heinemann himself.

"It's simple," he had told Mac. "Don't call him. If he calls, have Cramar tell him you're not there. Let it all go through me."

So Dobbs had called twice this morning. He shut the calendar with impatience and turned to his work.

The office quieted with Pat's departure for lunch. Outside sounds seeped into his consciousness, the keening of a foghorn, the stutter of the digital clock slotting new minutes into place. Muted by fog and distance, traffic sounds were almost indistinguishable.

The end of that silence came with the whining screech of tires failing to grip and the shattering, unmistakable crunch of metal on metal. Walter sat tensely, waiting for what must follow, shouts, expletives, anything please God. "Come on," he urged the silence crossly. "When car attacks car, human cries follow."

Nothing.

Pencil still in hand he leaned over Pat's desk to look into the parking lot. When the expletives began, they were his own.

An orange Volkswagen, hood elevated in astonishment, was inset into the side of his Porsche. He caught only an instant impression of a tall figure beside the cars before he was out of the door into the lot.

The girl turned at his approach. He didn't really see her at all, only brushing past, cursing silently, to examine the damage. The damned bug had clipped his fender, bending it inward to the wheel, wounding the lovingly polished silver with a deep stain of hideous orange.

"What in the name of God," he began, turning to her. She wasn't a girl but a woman. Middle to late thirties he decided.

Something in her stance stilled him. How could she stand so immobile and relaxed, her eyes full and thoughtful on him? The wind that stirred the fog took her hand to her forehead to brush back soft curls teased into her face. The translucence of her skin was relieved by the faintest dusting of pale freckles across her upper cheekbones.

"Is this your car?" she asked, too quietly for the magnitude of what had happened.

"Yes," Walter choked out somehow, wishing she were a man, wanting to hit her. "For the love of God, what were you doing?"

"Looking for a potter," she replied, almost physically withdrawing from his tone.

"A potter, for Christ's sake," he exploded. "In a marina?"

"I am sincerely sorry. It was such a beautiful car."

The past tense unnerved him.

"Damn right it was a beautiful car." He took the VW keys she held out. It didn't help that the reverse gear on the thing was elusive. Only after repeated grinding was he able to back the bug from his own car.

"Is it badly hurt?" she asked.

"Probably no more than five hundred dollars' worth," he replied acidly. "But it will never be the same. They never are. You are insured of course?"

She shrugged. "I suppose so. It was rented. But it doesn't matter."

"Doesn't matter?" he challenged. "What in hell does that mean?" The Porsche's crumpled fender turned his stomach. In spite of this gut reaction he realized he had overstated the damage. It was too late to recant.

"I'll pay whatever it costs," she explained. "I am very sorry." Her voice was so suddenly subdued that he had a moment of terror that she might cry.

"Not half as sorry as I am," he grumbled, a little gentler. "Let me park that bug for you."

She stood silently as he jockeyed the VW into Crane's stall. The telephone jangled inside the office. As he started for the door he kept seeing all the Plymouths he had owned. All those years he had continued buying Plymouths when it was a Porsche he wanted. He had felt that an agent should keep a low profile. Wouldn't you know? Eight months after he made the plunge for the Porsche a damned broad had to ram a rented VW into it. And orange.

The girl followed and waited meekly by Pat's desk as he took the call. She might be sorry, but she sure as hell wasn't nervous. Walter's breakfast tomato juice made tentative rising blazes toward his throat like mercury in a thermometer. She stood relaxed, gripping a purse of muted green and gold scraps sewn together. He forced his eyes away to concentrate on Mrs. Prescott.

Yes, the yawl's color would be one that people would notice right away. No, he didn't feel that genuine leather was practical for the finish of the cabin seats. Yes, Mrs. Prescott. No, Mrs. Prescott. Through all this the Porsche stared at him from the parking lot with that fender raised in reproach.

It wasn't the girl herself who irritated him but the cool way she waited when he couldn't get a grip on himself. "I'm over it now," he promised himself. "I'll be calm and quiet." The tranquillity in her face blew his resolve. She was annoyingly beautiful bathed in the light from the window. The muted green leather of her coat turned her eyes that same color. The perfection in the lines of her face stalled his words.

"You're a tourist, I presume," he said, turning to her.

She met his eyes serenely. "I'm visiting," she countered.

He looked for paper in Pat's desk only to have a dozen sheets of bond fan out and airplane across the floor.

"That figures," he said, trying two pens before remembering the pencil behind his ear. "Every spring it's the same. People come from everywhere to crowd our streets, block our driveways, jam our restaurants and drive their rented cars into ours."

When she remained silent, he waited, pencil poised. "Your name, please."

"Christa Cove, two C's."

"Address."

"Alta Mira Hotel."

"Not where you are staying," he said, "Where you live." He glanced up to see her staring with absorption through the window at the bay.

"Look, Mrs. Cove." His voice rose in spite of his best intentions. "I am a busy man. I have a lunch appointment. My whole day has been shot to bloody hell because of your damned potter. Do you mind giving me your identification so we can get this over with?"

He had mentally labeled her a dumb broad. When she turned like that he knew he was wrong. Stupid she wasn't. A glint in her eyes changed them from green to an indisputable gold, strange eyes, glowing as if from within. She laid out a card carrier opened to her driver's license. Her face stared back from the case, smiling. He hadn't seen her smile, he realized irrelevantly.

"Be my guest," she said quietly. "Actually I wasn't looking for a potter at all. I took my vacation, flew out here, rented a car and drove all over town to find your stinking little Porsche to goose just to be screamed at by a chauvinist bastard like you. What charisma you have."

He was caught in a startled stare.

"Doesn't your literacy extend to copying printed matter?" she prodded quietly.

He flushed and copied the data quickly. The address was obviously an apartment. Arlington, Virginia. He'd guessed her age pretty close and she was five eight, 115 pounds.

As she retrieved the case she handed him a check that he hadn't realized she was writing. It was made to bearer for five hundred dollars.

"Wait until the car is fixed," he protested. She was already half out of the door and the phone jangled imperiously at his elbow.

Jesus. He felt five inches tall.

"Did I get the day or the hour wrong?" his accountant asked against a hum of voices and glasses that Walter guessed was the bar at the Spinakker.

"Hell, no," Walter barked. "Some broad just creamed my car."

"Not the Porsche?" Ed asked with honest dismay.

"What else?"

"Should I come for you or change the date?" Ed's tone was solicitous.

"It'll run," Walter admitted. "If you'll drop me off, I'll leave it at the shop after lunch. It looks like hell. I'll be along right away. Have one on me."

"I already have," Ed admitted. "Several, in fact."

The sea fog had cleared. The sun blazed on the back of his neck on the way to the Spinakker. He was conscious of the bent fender and his own miserable performance. Boy, had she turned tiger. How could anyone look so serene and have a boiling point like that? He had lost his cool and behaved like a boor, like an American, he admitted morosely. By letting his emotions get the upper hand, he had mishandled the whole scene.

And now he had her damned check. He'd leave it at the Alta Mira as soon as he got an estimate on the repairs. He could only excuse himself that the calls from Dobbs had set him on edge.

And he still had to call the bastard back after two.

8

Blakeslea, California, April 25

Mac found himself haunted by the Sutter boy those following days. Not that he had a chance to forget about it, if he could have. The newspapers played the story complete with violins. The picture spreads were cleverly designed to portray ranchers and sprayers as the villains of the piece. The young parents, long-faced with grief, were shown huddled helplessly in hospital corridors. The mother was young and thin haired, struggling against tears. A toddler clawed at her disarray. They even ran a shot of the Robbins orchard next to the trailer lot as if the mature trees had sprung up overnight to threaten the frail mobile housing. In the picture you could read "DANGER DO NOT ENTER" even in the smudged newspaper print. The date was indistinct, but Mac knew it was there. The boy had clearly trespassed within the posted period.

"What more can a rancher do?" the sheriff was quoted.

"Robbins is in the business of raising fruit. He can't baby-sit for trespassers."

Mac threw the paper aside in disgust.

What had happened was plain enough even in the slanted story. The mother had turned the boy out without supervision and given no thought as to how he would amuse himself. He had been poisoned more by her negligence than the greed of any rancher.

He remembered Meg in and out of the door like a jumping jack when Toby was that age. He was never even in the park across the street without Meg stiff on a bench, raising her eyes from flashing knitting needles to watch him fly from seesaw to slide. He remembered evenings alone as she sat on the stoop watching him play along the street in the gathering dusk.

Early that week the last of the fertilizing was finished and the seeding began in earnest. Thursday Manuel was late with his truck. The phone was pealing before Mac's coffee water was hot.

"Jesus," Manuel breathed dolefully. "I got four tires all the way down. What I do now?"

"Where in hell did you park that crate?" Mac asked. Then quietly, "That kid of yours didn't have it out, did he?"

"No way," Manuel insisted. "This look like knives."

"Who in hell would knife four truck tires?" Mac asked, but he knew.

So that's how it was going to be. Cramar had mentioned pickets by the hospital. He hadn't thought of vandalism, but it was the next natural step. After sending a spare set of tires out to Manuel, he reported the damage to the sheriff and got his day off to a late and bitter start.

That same afternoon the Sutter child died. The announcement came on the droning radio in Cramar's office.

"Shut that damned thing off," Mac shouted, then growled. "Never mind, let it be." Listening, he found his gaze fixed on the key with the yellow tag hanging on the board by his desk.

The man he felt the sorriest for was Forrest Lamar. It was Lamar who had sprayed that fruit and Lamar was the granddaddy of them all. When Mac had come out to the valley to set up on his own, Lamar had talked a rancher into selling him the land to put his strip on.

"Competition hell," Lamar had said genially when Mac thanked him. "This valley is just beginning to develop. With the human race breeding like aphids it'll take more planes than all the flyboys in this country can keep in the air to feed those millions."

Now Lamar was in for one of those long drawn-out suits that made lawyers rich after any accident. For every trespasser who ignored a posting there were ten dollar-eager attorneys trying to trump up a punitive law suit.

Lamar would win because he was a man who took all the precautions. But he and Robbins, who owned the orchard, would both come out stained with the sorrow of the child's death. He'd go see Lamar, that's what he'd do. He was no damned slave to the shop or the rice season. It was only decent to go over and run up the flag for Lamar.

"I'm going into town for a bit," he told Cramar. "Mind covering until I get back?"

She nodded without looking up. As he swung his game leg down the stairs, she called after him. "Tell Lamar we are all hanging in there."

"Go to hell," he said, grinning back at her.

The sheriff was just leaving Lamar's as Mac pulled in.

"Scouting the opposition?" the sheriff asked.

Mac scowled. "We're all in this together. Is there going to be much more trouble?"

"No more than we can handle. I put three extra men on with the city force. It's the same old crowd, more posters than teeth."

"You don't flatten tires with posters," Mac reminded him.

The sheriff nodded. "Park close to the lights for a few days. We're checking out your damage."

Lamar rose as Mac entered. "Half expected you, Mac. Mowbrey was by a bit ago."

"Sheriff here on business?" Mac asked, accepting the chair Lamar nudged toward him.

Forrest Lamar passed his hand over that long wind-dried face the way he did. Lamar had been an agricultural pilot since he was twenty-three. That put him close to the start of the action. Years of crouching in an open cockpit plane had wrinkled his head and neck like a tortoise's.

"We lost a little window glass last night," he admitted. "They tried to turn over a plane, but the watchdogs drove them off."

"This is a hell of a way to make a living," Mac said.

"We're fighting bad memories," Lamar told him. "When did you last bite into a worm in an apple or find a straight tunnel dug through a head of cabbage? If we had a generation of people who fought the bugs for food and lost like they used to, we'd be sung heroes."

Mac rose. "Anything I can do to help?"

"You just did it," Lamar told him. "And I thank you."

His way back through town led Mac within a block of the hospital. The pickets had moved to the Valley Mortuary. There must have been twenty of them, pacing slowly back and forth before the immaculately tailored lawn. They wore sheets daubed with catsup to simulate blood. From a block away Mac could read the slogans on their placards. "The slaughter of innocents . . . when will it stop?"

He turned off Blake Avenue to avoid the pickets. Being that close he drove over to the lot he had bought when he first came out. The trees along the back had grown since his last visit. He parked the truck and paced the length of his land and then the width. Two new houses had gone up in the neighborhood. The one next door had been newly fenced. Bright plastic toys and a sandbox testified to the child whose world this had become. The swing was a low hung tire like Toby had when he was a kid.

73

A good neighborhood for kids.

If he had a house on his lot and Meg had been fool enough to take that kid, this would be a good place for her to be with him. No heavy fuel bills, lots of sunshine and himself close enough to look over them. Hell. He turned and stamped back to the truck. He didn't even know what Meg had done about the brat. It wasn't like Meg to hold her cards that close to her chest. Or it hadn't been in the old days.

When he got to Mary's Steakhouse, the old girl herself was tending bar. Her beehive looked freshly lacquered and she was wiping the bar with a rag that smelled like Christmas. He strained to see what she was putting on the rag. A smell like that might even cover the stench of tobacco smoke in his own trailer.

"You're not what I'd call rushed," he said as she drew him a beer.

"Too late for the early regulars and too early for the late," she explained. Mac was startled to realize that the hairs of her lashes seemed to be painted separately like a row of curved thistles.

He listened to her shout his order for ribs to the kitchen crew, then commented, "Lots of excitement in town tonight."

Mary nodded. "That rabble don't mean much to us out here. You don't buy booze when you're drunk on causes. It is tough about that kid though. His folks ought to be hauled in for criminal neglect."

"Tough on Forrest Lamar too."

She glanced up. "I heard some vandals hit out there. Having trouble at your place?"

"Some slashed tires," Mac said, handing his mug back for a refill. "So far that's all."

"I meant before all this," Mary said.

"What did you have in mind?" Mac countered.

Mary shrugged and started polishing glasses. "Just a feel I got from the way your Flying Mick guys gang up in here with that new guy, the tall, skinny one."

"I don't have any new guys," he protested. "Not since way back when we added the new planes."

"Don't jump me like that," Mary protested. "I just see this guy hanging out with your crowd and figured you'd signed him on. You know me, I never miss a new face if it happens to have a man fastened onto it."

"What's he like again?" Mac asked. The girl from the kitchen handed him the ribs wrapped to go.

Mary was frowning thoughtfully. "Tall, skinny, face like a buzzard. He has an accent. Say, Linda." The girl turned and waited. "What do they call that big drink of water that hangs out with the Flying Mick crowd?"

"Tex," the girl said quickly. "From his talk I'd say."

"And he's around here a lot with my men?" Mac asked.

"Not what you'd call a lot," Mary revised. "Once in a while I see him with that partner of yours, the one who came on last."

Dobbs. Mac's beer soured in his mouth. He paid up and slid a tip across the wet bar.

"Now that's why I prefer an Irishman to a Scot." Mary grinned at him, taking the money. But Mac noticed she put it into the bartender's bowl instead of her own pocket.

Mac ground the truck into gear. So that's how it was. Dobbs had a spy around town, a big, hawk-nosed Texan who hung around with the men. That explained how Dobbs learned so fast about the Sutter boy. It might even explain why Rick stayed on the prod so much. God only knew what Dobbs was feeding those guys, undermining him with his own crew. Mac slammed the steering wheel with his fist and then had to fight the truck back onto the road.

But that creep of cold stirred along his spine again. He was restless from the sense that just beyond the angle of his vision something was swinging silently like a scythe, back and forth, back and forth.

The smell of the ribs on the seat beside him made him a little sick. Dobbs. Always Dobbs. But why?

9

April 28

Walter Heinemann wakened to the moan of foghorns. He lay listening to Christa's even breathing before rising on an elbow to look at her.

She looked different in sleep. Her hair spread in soft mounds on the pillow, tendriling on her bared shoulders. With those green eyes closed, she seemed a sun-freckled child, remarkably vulnerable.

His hand moved toward her breast, whose nipple was half concealed by her tumbled hair. Checking himself, he eased from the bed, torn between desire for her and irritation at himself for becoming this involved emotionally with anyone, much less a girl he had met a bare two weeks before.

At his movement she sighed and turned. Walter froze until she settled again, her head back and one slender hand trailing off the bed, fingers half curled in sleep.

Her hands were like his mother's, lean, almost shapeless wrists, pale veining and wide, flat nails with deeply striated moons.

With his robe around his nakedness he stood at the railing overlooking the bay. California was pleasant in climate and dramatic in terrain, but a hostile planet compared to the remembered green of his homeland. Only the bay reminded him of home. His adult mind failed to recall any flaws of Lithuania, its flowing, green pastures silvered with birches, endless sunlight strident with birdsong.

But the blue of the bay recalled the Baltic Sea even as Christa's hands brought memories of his mother. He had seen his mother's hands curled in rest even as Christa's were, but he had never seen his mother in sleep. His parents' bedroom was a forbidden and mysterious world. From that doorway the light seemed diffused and pink from the dark red hangings. The mirror, viewed obliquely, reflected massive, dark furniture, the memory of which evoked fear and confusion.

He must have been five or six that summer. Although he had been in bed for hours, small birds still rustled outside his window and shafts of light moved uncertainly across his polished floor. But the day had felt unfinished. His father, expected for the evening meal, had never come. Two places still sat reproachfully with a handful of flowers and wine glasses on the dining table.

He was startled awake by his father's voice, rough with anger. He had staggered toward the door only to be greeted by silence. The white coverlet of their bed was undisturbed. He had sought his mother in terror through the darkened house. In the dining room one of the glasses had been half filled with red wine and then abandoned.

He was whimpering with relief when he found her in the garden. She sat with bowed head, her hand trailing like Christa's. Her attitude spelled defeat. For a moment he thought her dead, her flesh so translucent, her hand so emptied of life.

Even her clothes seemed untenanted, discarded garments limp in the chair.

When she saw him it was with a cry.

"Walter." Then he was in her arms. Her body was a blaze of warmth and her arms seemed endless, folding away the night and the chill and the terror of his search.

He had pulled back to stare at her. "Are you all right?"

"All right," she assured him with a quick false laugh. "How could I be otherwise with you here? I am tired, Walter. That is all, only very tired."

"But I heard shouting."

"Your father was tired too," she explained. "The strikes, the peasants." Her voice had trailed off. She rose and picked him up. "What a great bundle you are," she jested. "An old, tired mother has to haul you like fresh laundry."

"I can walk," he protested, but she held him tightly.

"One day you shall carry me," she said, laughing. "Tonight is my time."

She had sat by his bed until he heard the scrape of his father's step. Then she pulled away, smoothing her dress. Her embrace left the fine, spicy scent of her in his head for a long time.

He had never carried his mother, he thought bitterly, not even in any symbolic way. He had not even protected her. By the time the Germans came he understood the forces that separated his parents, his father's Prussian pragmatism against the half-Catholic, tree-worshiping mysticism of his mother. Betrothed as a child, she had matured to rebel against this invader of her body as her people had rebelled for so many centuries against Vikings, Slavs, Mongols and finally the Germans.

At seventeen he had fled the advancing German armies to take arms against them in Russia. Why had he dreamed that the gentle women of Lithuania would be safe from their barbarism?

Nearly half of the Luftwaffe had been in Russia that spring

of 1942. There had been neither time nor strength to dwell on Vilna.

A covy of sailboats left the yacht harbor to move delicately down Richardson Bay. Not since his mother and her pointless, brutal death had any woman entangled him like this Christa Cove, whom he had met in rage and now adored like a hot-eyed adolescent.

He told himself he sought her to return the check, but he knew he was deluding himself. The clerk at the Alta Mira refused the envelope. "Miss Cove has checked out. I have no forwarding address."

"What of her mail?" Walter insisted.

The clerk showed him the register with the same Arlington address he had copied from her permit.

"Then *how* did she go?" he pressed. "Rented car? Taxi?"

"Try the valet service," the man suggested. "They generally know more than we do."

"Cove," the man repeated, frowning. "Tall, good-looking, loud VW?"

Walter nodded. "Any idea where she went?"

"Yeah," the man nodded as if surprised himself. "She was pretty chatty. Told me a friend was subletting an apartment for a while. She showed me the address and asked how to get there."

The Porsche complained at the slow climb up Bulkely Street. Once Walter pulled off to let a truculent driver pass. The last apartment at the top of the hill, the valet had told him. The unit was built over a rank of carports. The third from the end held the orange VW.

By the time he locked the car's wheels against the incline and stood at the doorbell it was after six, a damned inconvenient time for a call.

Christa didn't answer until the third ring. Walter was poised for departure when she finally opened the door. Standing there barefooted, she was shorter than he remembered. Her hair was caught loose and high, the fringe of curls escaping over her forehead giving her a gamin look. She was wearing something loose and scarlet, roped at the waist with a tasseled cord. She stared at him over the dripping wooden spoon she held over her curved palm.

"Be quick," she ordered. "You are spoiling my ciorba."

The scent had been vague on the doorstep. In the open doorway it was overpowering, garlic and peppers and fish and something acidic. "Spoiling what?" he asked.

"Good God," she said crossly, then backed off, still sheltering the spoon from spoiling the rug. "Ciorba, soup, come on in."

He had followed her to the kitchen, which was dense with steam. She ignored him as she examined two thick white fish steaks poaching in a French skillet and stirred a sauce simmering on another burner. Then she sighed, satisfied, and lifted the steaks onto an earthenware dish. "They are easily overcooked," she explained as she slid the dish into the oven. "They go all to mush. Now, what do you want?"

She shoved back the fringe of curls, obviously impatient.

He groped for his wallet. "Your check," he explained. "Remember? My Porsche, your VW? It was too much money."

A smile teased her lips. "But it will never be the same," she mimicked in his petulant tone.

"I'm sorry. I do apologize. I was overwrought."

"I understand," she assured him. "It was a beautiful car. Is it all right again?"

"Perfectly," Walter told her. Her glance strayed from him to the stove where the puree was simmering by the chopping board mounded with diced cucumbers.

"Would you care for a glass of wine?" she asked.

"You're awfully busy," he protested, tempted.

She shrugged. "The dangerous part is over. I have a few minutes now."

While she brought the wine, Walter grinned to himself.

"Dangerous." He could hardly feel threatened by a woman who found a poaching fish a matter of peril.

The wine was very cold and remarkably fragrant. "So they were able to fix your car perfectly," she said almost mockingly.

Nodding, he laid the check on the table.

She stared at him. "They didn't repair it for nothing."

"A nominal fee," he told her. "And there was insurance."

"I have no intention of falling into your debt," she told him. Her rising inflection suggested warning.

"Actually, Miss Cove, I feel more as if I were in your debt."

Not until her face dimpled with laughter did the pomposity of his own words hit him.

"Goddammit, woman," he exploded into laughter. "For some idiot reason you bring out the pompous ass in me."

She smiled as she refilled his glass. "I don't know what the going rate is for ten minutes of absolute boorishness," she admitted.

"One Porsche fender," he suggested.

She was staring at him thoughtfully. "Do you like fish?"

"Immensely," he replied. Good God, couldn't she keep her mind on anything for ten seconds running?

"Then I shall serve dinner to you," she said. "That should even the score." Then she paused. "Unless you have an engagement, a wife, a lover?"

"No engagement," he admitted. "But quite an imposition on you."

"I am only paying back that nominal fee," she reminded him. "Only I do it in Romanian."

She was handing him a bewildering array of articles, place mats, ornate silver, fringed napkins. "You are Romanian then?" he asked.

"Lipovan," she corrected. "Northern Romania, along the delta. I have been away forever and yet I hunger for that food."

"The wine can't be Romanian."

"Alsatian," she agreed. "Edzelwicker."

He watched as she finished the meal, wondering how any meal so simple could be so memorable. She placed the drained fish steaks in wide, deep bowls, which she served with a sauceboat of mingled soup and garlic paste. Then, with the cucumber in the soup, she tasted, salted and ladled it over the fish.

"Delicious," he admitted at the first bite. She passed him the breadbasket, beaming.

She was remarkably easy to talk to. He found himself describing the pike from the Neris River in Vilna and how his mother had them prepared. She told him of her days in the gymnasium in Budapest after her parents "disappeared" and she became the foster daughter of an army couple.

After the cheese and fruit and well-aged red wine, Walter decided that the fender on the Porsche had been one of his better investments. How well he knew her already, and yet so sketchily.

What did she do? "I am a scientist," she had replied soberly.

"What kind of a scientist?" he had probed.

"One does not discuss work on a holiday," she rebuked him, fitting her slender body against his own.

A holiday. A visitor. She was an eel with his questions. How long would she stay? That careless shrug. Yet the thought of her leaving brought a dull pain. What if she stayed? Was there a place in his life for a woman? Many women perhaps, but not one.

He glanced to see her watching him from her pillow. The peculiar contrast between her serenity of body and vivacity of expression roused him.

"You left me," she said when he went to her. "Don't you realize how much longer the day is than the night?"

With the drapes closed, her eyes gleamed that incandescent green.

Her body was pliant. Only her hands were cool.

A teasing smile always lingered on her face after lovemaking. She still wore that smile after they had marketed and stowed the picnic hamper in his boat for a day on the bay.

He was maneuvering the boat from its slot when she called for his attention. "Is that man trying to hail you?" she asked.

He shaded his hands against the glare. Stanley Dobbs was on the dock, waving and shouting.

"Oh, God," he muttered.

"You can pretend he's not there," she suggested.

"It's your fault for telling me," he told her. "Now I am into it."

Once at the dock, Dobbs was apologetic. "I'm really sorry," he told Walter, eyeing Christa curiously. "I was on my way down to look at a plane for sale when they reached me. It's another flap out at the Flying Mick."

"Another what?" Walter challenged curtly. Surely Dobbs didn't think of the death of the little Sutter boy as a "flap."

"Another accident," Dobbs explained. "At the field. Rick piled up."

"Again?" Walter asked angrily.

Dobbs flushed. "Don't jump to conclusions. I just thought we should check it out. It sounded pretty bad."

"Then you're going up?" Walter asked.

"Hell, yes," Dobbs said.

Walter sighed. Dobbs's car was parked crossways behind the marina stalls. Another man waited in the car, a tall, dark-haired man watching the regatta out in the bay.

"Well?" Dobbs urged, looking at Christa again.

"I'll come up," Walter said. "You go on ahead. I'll be along."

By the time the boat was back in its moorings Christa had carried everything up from below. A triangle of scarf fluttered around her face as she braced herself between the hamper and the cooler of wine.

"I'm ready," she told him.

"This could be nasty," he warned.

"I've only found your company nasty once," she told him. "It might be fun for old times' sake."

He grinned at her. Dobbs and his companion had left. He leaned to find her lips soft under his. He caught her lower lip with his teeth and held it, feeling the firmness of her back beneath his hand as he pulled her close.

"It smells like death out there where we are going," he warned her again.

"I have been to Los Angeles," she told him, touching her injured lip reproachfully with her tongue.

"You talk like a native San Franciscan," he said as they hauled their picnic back to his car.

10

April 28

Back on the highway with Tex Jackson beside him, Dobbs fell silent. Where had he seen that green-eyed girl of Walter's before? It had been recently, just the past few weeks. He remembered the face and the strange eyes without being able to pin them to any setting. It must have been a party because his memory was tinged with something more sensual and flowing than the sunny, outdoor impression she gave from the deck of Heinemann's boat.

But it had to be the same girl. There couldn't be two like that, lean, supple body topped by odd-colored hair and those eyes. Like his own Ginger, a little maturity hadn't hurt her but rather enhanced the appeal of a naturally beautiful package.

He glanced over at Jackson's hawklike profile at his side. The quality of restless strength in Jackson amazed him. Even with both arms folded over the jacket in his lap, Jackson looked like a man coiled to spring. He had a quick head with a slow tongue, a damned good combination. He was exactly the right man. But how in hell was he going to unseat Mac?

The bay dropped away behind them as Dobbs gunned the car north.

"Too bad the call came before we got to try out that plane," Dobbs remarked. "But I'm damned glad Ginger knew where to reach me. God only knows what we'll find at the Flying Mick."

"Maybe we'll get lucky," Jackson suggested.

Dobbs glanced at his watch. A quarter after twelve. The call had been a little garbled through no fault of Ginger's. She didn't even know the name of the pilot who had called from Blakeslea to report that Rick had crashed a plane.

Dobbs's own call to the field had been scarcely more helpful. Cramar's voice had been shrill and frantic. A standpipe, she said. Rick had plowed into a standpipe. The ground crew had radioed from the site for an ambulance. Mac wasn't around. Dobbs heard the droning of planes behind her voice as she talked.

If it hadn't taken so long to run down that damned Heinemann, they would be at the site by now.

"If it's Rick you're worrying about, you might as well leave that for the medics," Jackson said quietly.

Dobbs nodded. It was neither Rick nor the plane that kept his foot firm on the gas pedal. Naturally he was sorry if Rick had banged himself up, but the guy had been a whining troublemaker from the first. It was Mac he wanted to confront. An accident a week? God. What kind of a manager ran a shop that sloppy?

He had taken the time to chase Heinemann down in the hope that he would drive up with them. His words would have a lot more impact if he arrived with Heinemann, like buddies. The blonde had spoiled that.

"I know that girl," Dobbs mused aloud.

"The one at the boat?" Jackson asked. "A dish from my distance."

Dobbs nodded. "My partner lives well."

A Stearman bellied them on approach as Dobbs pulled into the lot. Business as usual. A ground crew was reloading a truck, and the electrical whine rose and fell from Evert's shop. Jackson, breathing the fetid air, coughed and spat and laughed.

"Tastes like home." He grinned over at Dobbs.

Cramar looked even worse than usual. Her thin hair flew from its net above her reddened eyes. A wadded handkerchief was moist on her desk. She seized it to ball in her hands as he entered.

She had no more to tell but repeated it anyway. Her voice rose and fell in competition with the din outside.

"They won't tell you a thing at that hospital," she complained. "Mac's over there now. He'll know the most. For sure Rick's back is broke with maybe head injuries." She glanced at the clock. "He was into surgery a little before eleven. But they won't tell you nothing."

She trailed a pencil line across her map to show the field where the plane was downed. "Be sure and tell the sheriff who you are," she cautioned. "They don't cotton to sightseers around here."

The site was seven miles east of the strip. Pickups and trucks were parked a mile down the road with the circulating red light of an official car up ahead. Dobbs parked behind the last truck and they walked in.

A motley crowd, mostly local people, stared vacantly at the wreckage of the plane. The equipment was still there, a Flying Mick truck and a sick-looking flagger standing among the ranchers by the fence. The Stearman was upended like a beetle with the spraying tips on its wings clawing the air helplessly. One demolished wing lay several feet from the body of the plane. The sheriff approached them, eyeing Dobbs warily.

"Any word on the pilot?" Dobbs asked. "I'm one of the Flying Mick partners."

The sheriff relaxed and shook his head. "You just missed the FAA men. They got right on this. Pictures, the lot." His voice trailed off. "No word on the pilot yet."

"He was lucky to live clear to town," Jackson said, eyeing the wreckage.

Dobbs, leaning nearer the plane under the sheriff's watchful eyes, coughed from the stench of spilled fuel. An unreasoning surge of satisfaction filled him. Mac had had it now. This was no light accident but a killer.

"Where in hell is Heinemann?" he asked petulantly when the sheriff had moved out of earshot. "Mac is turning our business into a bone yard and he doesn't even show. It's easy enough to mouth any old excuse, a low wire, a standpipe. How in hell do we know that this plane was in fit condition to fly?"

"Or the pilot," Jackson reminded him. "There's always pilot error."

"Rick's an okay pilot," Dobbs protested. "Or he was until Mac got hold of him. Seven-day weeks, fourteen-hour days, what man can take that kind of punishment forever? You sure as hell don't see Mac laying a load like that on himself."

"You might say that again," Jackson drawled lazily.

Dobbs froze, struck by a sudden thought.

God in heaven. Had he seen or heard of Mac being in the air since his son, Toby, went down? Was this possible? If Mac had turned chicken on flying, he had the final snap on the case against him. Not even Heinemann would dare stand up for a chief pilot who hadn't the guts to check out his own planes.

Dobbs backed from the plane and hailed the sheriff. "I'd like to talk to the owner of this field."

"Down there," the sheriff pointed. "White with a green roof, just a couple of miles. They only left a bit ago."

"Mac's partner, eh?" the rancher said as he opened the door to Dobbs. "Always glad to meet a friend of Mac's." His wife, a genial woman with cinnamon-colored hair, offered them iced tea.

"Don't want to waste your time," he told them. "I just wanted to tell you how sorry I am that this happened in your field."

The man shook his head. "These things happen. Mac's insurance always covers. It's the flier we fret about. Pray God he gets okay. That's a standard field," he added a little nervously.

"So the Flying Mick has done your work before?" Dobbs asked.

"Oh, hell, yes, five years or more now. Never a complaint. Great fellow that Mac. But this here field is a new one. We just put it in."

"But Mac checked it out before he sent the crew in?"

"Sure thing. Came out the day I called about fertilizing it. He went all over it and wrote a bunch of stuff down."

"Then he flew it?" Dobbs pressed.

The rancher shook his head. "Never flew it, just walked it with the flagman, making notes, hedges and all."

"Had a sandwich with us when he was done," his wife added. "We had a fresh-cut ham as I remember."

Dobbs caught Jackson's eyes on his own, that clear cold blue gaze. It was an intimate glance, cool and amused.

He had Mac now. By God, he had Mac cold.

We should think rather on what we shall do than what we shall say: when we have decided on that, it will be easy enough to accommodate our words to our act.

Niccolò Machiavelli,
The Discourses,
Chapter XV

Part TWO

11

Ciudad Juarez, April 27

The printed cotton shirt that Igor Grigoryev had selected as a convincing costume for an American on a Mexican holiday turned out to be one of those synthetic blends that cut off all air. Inside that buttoned prison his torso streamed with a salty torrent of sweat that soaked into his limp trousers and forced his socks into damp lumps around his ankles.

There was little traffic on the pedestrian bridge that led from El Paso in Texas to the city of Juarez. Young couples tossed coins to divers in the Rio Grande as birds of prey wheeled above the mountain beyond. Love and death. Igor forced his mind back to his mission. Even to let his mind stray was to skirt the unthinkable.

Ciudad Juarez. Igor opened the tourist guide he had bought in El Paso. While seeming to study the pages, his eyes searched the other walkers on the bridge. Relieved, he stowed the book and set off for the city market.

"Cigarette?" A boy cried at his elbow. The urchin jammed the pack into his face, a rectangle closely resembling a popular American brand. From the alacrity with which he pulled it back, Igor guessed that the cigarettes were bogus, some local weed wrapped to resemble the real thing.

"*No fumare,*" Igor grumbled, waving the boy away. The boy followed, his bare feet slapping on the hot sidewalk. "Divorce?" the boy urged eagerly. "Fine quick divorce? False teeth?"

The boy's face was close enough to infect Igor with whatever evil germs the child might host. "Get lost," he shouted, perversely proud of this automatic Americanism.

The street stunk of people, women whose perfumed bodies suggested meat that had been sugared without being cured. At least he should be able to stay on the miserable diet his doctor had given him. How could a man be tempted to eat in a place still ablaze with his memories of the last bout of *turista* he had endured?

At the stoplight he mopped his face. Jesus, it was hot. What a hellhole Vladimir had chosen for this meeting. Had the vindictive old bastard guessed he was torturing a dying man?

Two weeks had passed since their meeting in Quebec City. His agent had been in California and on the job within twenty-four hours of his own return to Washington. What other agent could have produced so appropriate an agent for this job so quickly? Even Vladimir had to be impressed with the report Igor had relayed. God knows that it was neither Igor's fault nor that of his agent that the report had been, in the end, indecisive.

But damn it all, why hadn't his agent simply tossed a coin to choose between Heinemann and Dobbs? Heads you live, tails you die. No matter how punctual and immaculate the report was, it still left the decision unmade and both agents in place.

Igor had read and reread those reports with anguish. Stanley Dobbs (born Drobot) was a stinking paragon. His motivation was ideological, born of his fervent desire to overthrow the enemies of the Russian peasant class. The man was too rich to be bought. His habits were normal, an ordinary drinker, no addictions, a discreet but heterosexual life, no professional vulnerability. He was cunning, ruthless and flexible.

"You could hardly expect a careful agent to eliminate such a man," he thought defensively. The unremitting sun was making his chronic headache worse. When the headache first began, he had referred to the tattered medical dictionary on his desk.

"Probably only a symptom," the book stated. The list of possible causes of this symptom (disorder in alimentary tract, toxemia, the onset of febrile disease) had sent him flying to his physician.

Instead of an airy diagnosis and a handful of pills, the doctor had hauled him through every painful test those overpaid sadists had ever devised. Only to come to the end that sent a shudder of disbelief down his anguished body. He couldn't let himself think about that. Even touching it with his mind was out.

A block ahead, flags fluttered at the city market. Involuntarily his steps slowed. What if Vladimir forced him to make the selection? How could he choose without flipping a coin?

Walter Heinemann. Good Christ. If Dobbs was an angel, then Walter was God himself. Motivation: hatred and revenge following the murder of his mother in a Nazi camp. Unmarried, industrious, clever and discriminating. His political future seemed assured with the momentum he had already established sufficient to carry him to the state, possibly even the national political level.

A bare two weeks remained before the deadline Vladimir had given him. Both men still lived, risking minute-to-minute mutual disclosure through their connection to that damned dusting company.

Once inside the market, the piles of fruits and vegetables

gave way to extravaganzas of paper flowers, woven baskets and piñatas hanging above his head. The odor of food was overpowering, a sharpness of chilis, the heaviness of hot fat. The cries of the merchants blended with a mariachi band to produce a deafening roar.

Thank God he knew where Vladimir would be. Affecting nonchalance, he moved to the appointed booth.

The stench of cigar smoke flowed from behind the curtain as Igor leaned to inspect a tray of turquoise rings whose massive stones were surrounded by an offensive trim. The merchant's invitation was casual.

"Many more in back, señor," he purred. The man's teeth were edged with plaque. "Fit for queen, señor, your queen."

Vladimir's great body was poised on a raffia stool. He removed his cigar as Igor entered. His hand was amber from smoke.

"I have the report," he said tersely. His tone was caustic. "It is not conclusive," he added, openly hostile.

"The agent is a trained psychologist," Igor replied. "The best of credentials. The assignment was for a nonclinical assessment of the two men."

Vladimir coughed and cleared his throat. For one sickening moment, Igor imagined that mucous landing in the dust at his feet. Instead, Vladimir withdrew a handkerchief and cleaned his mouth.

"The assignment was to be completed in thirty days," he reminded Igor. "Only half of that time is left."

"That's why I sent you the report with all speed," Igor said. "If it is to come to tossing a coin between the two men . . ."

"Tossing a coin?" Vladimir interrupted in disbelief.

"A jest," Igor said hastily.

"A good man acts," Vladimir said angrily. "He acts first and then frames his words with explanation. Machiavelli teaches that . . . but to a world where few are eager to learn."

Igor could feel the slow cadence of his own death march as

he breathed the tainted air of the confined booth. Once he might have feared demotion from Vladimir's anger. What was demotion now?

Astonishingly, Vladimir's tone turned gentle. "I have taken this responsibility for you, Igor. After careful study of our own future plans, I have arranged to have Stanley Dobbs notified by his handler to eliminate Walter Heinemann." His tone was silken with satisfaction as he shrugged. "Too bad about Heinemann of course, but all men die in time."

Igor's breath stopped in his throat.

"That's true enough, isn't it, comrade?" Vladimir prodded. "How much grander to go down in strength than turn to babbling on a couch without wit or discretion."

"Without wit or discretion." Such a man would be released from his pain quick enough for the sake of security. Did Vladimir know what rottenness coiled in Igor's own belly?

He could only nod at Vladimir's searching glance.

"So it is settled," Vladimir said.

Igor struggled for a firmness of breath, hoping the question would not be considered presumptuous. "What part does my agent play in this now?"

Vladimir laughed. "What Americans call an observer. To remain in place, watch the execution and congratulate Stanley Dobbs."

Igor was startled. "Why expose an agent like that?"

"It is presumed that Dobbs will have arranged a death that leaves no trace of his own guilt. It is important that he know that we are privy both to the act and the means. One never misses an opportunity to increase leverage on an agent this far from the homeland."

The meeting was over. Vladimir rose with an almost jovial expression. Looking down on Igor in that cramped space, he laughed.

"It is proper for you to feel concern about your part in this operation. A stalemate is not a win, Igor. But in the end this might turn out well for us. Stanley Dobbs might even be worth what he is costing us in losing Heinemann."

"I hope your health is better than usual," he added as an afterthought.

"Fine, comrade," Igor insisted, straightening himself purposely. "And yours the same I hope."

Vladimir's eyes missed nothing. He laughed at this new, stiff posturing. "My health is never less than fine," he reminded him.

When ten minutes had elapsed, Igor emerged from the reeking back of the booth. The merchant smiled at him, still playing his game. "You have found something for your queen, señor?"

The meeting had gone badly. El Paso seemed painfully far away. The border lay between, and customs. He bought two piñatas, a giant red bull and a rabbit with a carrot in its mouth. Night was on the town. Whores called from doorways. His belly was a great melon seeded with death. Radium. Chemotherapy. Beyond surgery. The doctor's words were as useless as his pills. "Without wit or discretion."

A few blocks from the pedestrian bridge he paused at a restaurant window. The people within were well dressed and smiling and American. The lamp shone on the tables and floor. The place was clean, really clean.

A waiter passed the window bearing an oval tray where a red snapper lay bedded in crisp green, studded with radishes. The fish seemed to be smothered beneath a sauce of braised green olives and strips of red chili. Igor plunged through the door, a man compelled.

Igor argued his own case over the menu. Even a dying murderer orders a last meal. If a man must die by inches, why should he rob himself of any pleasure that he can find?

He would have guacamole with tostados, spicy with coriander instead of the garlic they used stateside. Chilis en Nogada, succulent chilis stuffed with beef and onion, moist with raisins, crisp with nuts and covered with cream.

He saw the faces of the two men in his mind. Dobbs had the look of a younger, slimmer Vladimir. Heinemann looked the sort of man he himself might have been, given better health all these years.

The waiter brought a Marguerita with the guacamole. Igor savored the crust of salt against his lips. The sweet blaze of seasoned tequila numbed his gut. To hell with Vladimir, who would issue the same kill order for him when the truth came out. The same careful words.

Wiping the last of the cream from his lips, he waved to the waiter for sopapillas. A dying man had no master but time.

No master. He stared at the golden puffs of pastry. At their side was a small pitcher of the fine honey of Mexico. Sweet and fulsome. Igor broke the sopapilla with a greedy finger and let the fine stream of honey feed into the hollowness.

There was still indecision. The habits of a lifetime do not change easily as the normal cells of his body had given over to the invading cancer.

The moment, the very moment that this proliferating rottenness in his belly delivered him over to those drugs that would rob him of wit and discretion, Vladimir would order him killed.

In the meantime there would be pain and the slow wasting.

The waiter was changing courses at the next table. He brought coffee in small cups and Tia Maria. The man leaned toward his girl whose dark eyes shone in the light of the candle. The cigar that her escort lit at the flame reeked of Vladimir.

The nausea began in Igor's beleaguered gut. Dead men had no masters. Life was a rigged race. There was no win, only place and show.

Would to God that some wisdom were available to man to abort fate. If only the Bible, his mother's book, or Machiavelli . . .

The fox. To play the fox. Igor smiled and cleansed a spot of honey from his palm with a moistened napkin. Let Vladimir lose for once; his turn was overdue. He knew the form that the execution order would take, having issued them himself. Let Stanley Dobbs die. By God let it be a race between them. In the end Vladimir would be found out and that would be winning.

"How much grander to go down in strength than babbling on a couch." Vladimir's own words, Vladimir's own style, Machiavellian.

"Go down in strength."

Igor paid his check with a light heart. He crossed the pedestrian bridge almost jauntily, swinging his piñatas like a tourist delighted with a glimpse of a new country.

12

Blakeslea Memorial Hospital, April 29

For the first few hours Mac had moved restlessly from one uncomfortable vinyl chair to another in the surgical waiting room at the Blakeslea Memorial Hospital. Finally, as an act of penance, he forced himself to stay in the same green chair where he would have to observe the results of his growing tension in the overfilled ashtray.

His head hummed from the steady pealing of phones from the station down the hall, the squeal of rubber shoes on polished tiles and the irony of hushed voices in this swirl of sound. Merely sitting there waiting for news of Rick was a trial to his spirit. Jesus. What had he done wrong with Rick? Sure, standpipes had brought more than one pilot down, good pilots with their heads screwed on. But for a man to have two accidents in one week, he had to be fighting something beside his plane. "I should have seen that," Mac told himself bitterly. "I should have grounded him until he was on top of whatever was bugging him."

The rumbling in his belly finally drove him from his chair to the hospital cafeteria downstairs. After the coffee he had made himself at dawn, he had wolfed down some rolls that Cramar brought in. Lunch had somehow been lost in the confusion of Rick's accident.

The cafeteria line with its hooded steam tables and white attendants clicked him back to those anguished days he had spent waiting for Meg to live or die after Toby's birth. That week had set him up for a lot of things. By its end he had accepted that all he and Meg would ever have as a family was this one jug-eared kid. Only much later did he realize that it had set Meg up to be so fiercely protective of that kid that she would sacrifice their marriage in the hope of keeping Toby from anything as dangerous as flying. If that wasn't enough, it had set him up to detest hospitals so much that he settled for a cardboard cup of lukewarm coffee that he could carry back to the waiting room.

He let the hands of the clock crawl another hour before he stopped the nurse again. She sighed at his approach. Her voice was acid with reproach.

"As I told you before, Mr. Maguire, we will have word only when the surgery is completed."

He swallowed his anger with difficulty. Feisty little bitch. He didn't trust any of them. They were a bunch of primitive witch doctors hiding their little mysteries behind those swinging doors.

"I'll be out at the airfield," he told her. "I'd appreciate someone calling the minute there's any word."

He almost turned north to catch a sandwich at Mary's Steakhouse but thought better of it. As sure as he stopped by, the hospital would call and he would miss the word. And the place would be filled with ranchers and their wives having late Sunday dinner. He didn't want to be asked any questions that he didn't have the answers for.

He was relieved to see Evert's car in the lot of the Flying Mick. They would have to get together right away on getting that plane put back into shape. He cursed at the dogs throwing themselves against the fence and limped into the trailer.

He shook his head at Cramar's questioning glance.

"Still in surgery," he told her. "And those tight-mouthed bitches would see you in hell before they'd give you the time of day. No word while I was driving out?"

She shook her head bleakly. "Dobbs came by with another fellow. I sent them on to the site of the wreck."

"And Heinemann?" he asked.

"He called in," Cramar replied. "Told me to tell you to hang in there, that he was on his way out."

He nodded and reached for the sheets piling up on his desk. They were already four hours behind schedule and no help coming.

"I saved you some lunch," she said after a minute. "In case you missed it in town."

He stared at her. "Saved him some lunch." He knew what she called lunch, what she carried in that canvas shoulder bag for herself—a leftover meat loaf sandwich and a plastic butter tub of cottage cheese. But it was the thought that counted, as Meg always said. "Hey," he said, trying to force some enthusiasm. "That's great because I'm starved."

To his amazement she reached under her desk to pull up a bag stained with the distinctive orange grease of the taco shop. The source of these stains were three rolled burritos, still faintly warm, and a taco whose refritoes had spilled out onto the waxed paper.

"Just some old leftovers, eh?" He grinned at her. She turned back to her desk swiftly. "What would you have done with these if I ate in town or hadn't come back?"

"I never saw anything yet those dogs out there wouldn't eat," she said, her voice revealing her satisfaction.

With the food boiling around inside him, Mac finished up at his desk and spent an hour in the shop with Evert. He was still there when Cramar shouted for him from the door of the trailer, her voice shrill against the roar of the Stearman being loaded on the strip.

"Hineyman on the phone," she shrieked. "I told him to hold."

"I'm at the hospital," Heinemann's crisp voice reported. "Rick is just coming out of surgery. I told them I'd call you."

"How does it look?" Mac asked.

"Not good," Heinemann admitted. "But he's still alive. And Dobbs is here."

"Jesus."

"I thought you might feel that way," Heinemann said mildly. "He says he's due back in Atherton early. Want me to let you know when he clears out?"

"That would be a help," Mac said dryly.

"Hang in there then. When he leaves, we'll be out."

"We?" Mac asked warily.

"I brought along a friend I was going sailing with," Heinemann explained. "Try to get squared away to have dinner with us."

"Check," Mac agreed, hanging up the phone.

Cramar was looking up at him bleakly.

"Like Heinemann says, the good news is that he's still breathing."

Mac stared dully at his desk. His Irish bones told him that Rick wasn't going to make it. A heaviness weighed on his mind as he shuffled the numbers Evert had given him out in the shop. Sure, they were only seat-of-the-pants numbers, hours of man work, cost of material, cost of replacement parts, but the total was even worse than Mac had feared. It would take a year to get that crate back in the air under the normal work schedule, three months if Evert didn't do a damned thing but that. Even if the plane were ready, who would fly it? The men always took tight loads because it meant more bread for each of them, but there was no way they could pick up Rick's time too.

Mac sighed. Now to get on the horn and bring in another

pilot with his own plane and pay him an arm and leg for it. Even that was better than letting down the ranchers lined up for the rest of the season.

Scavengers circled the place all afternoon. A crew from the Sacramento TV station literally followed the flatbed in from the field after the FAA had cleared it.

"We just aren't here," Mac told Evert, locking himself and Cramar into the office. "You fend those bastards off so I can get this work done."

It was after six when Heinemann called to say that Dobbs had finally left. It was Cramar who insisted that Mac agree to meet him and his friend at the steak house.

"I wasn't figuring on leaving until late anyway," she told him. "Take your time with dinner but call if there's any word on Rick."

"You owe yourself a healthy check for overtime," Mac said in lieu of thanks.

"I'll type it and you sign," she replied tartly. "My best to Mr. Hineyman."

The girl with Heinemann smiled as Mac approached. "Christa Cove," he repeated, surprised by the strength of her handshake.

She slid over. "Sit down. You've had a long day. The extra beer glass is for you."

The only thing he'd seen prettier than her all day was the amber stream she poured from the big glass pitcher.

"Dinner is on me tonight," Mac announced. "I intend to eat a man off his horse."

"You are snobbish about horsemeat then?" the girl teased, pointing to the menu with a slender finger. "That," she announced, "is what I'm having."

Mac laughed, feeling an easing of the tense muscles along his back. "Make that two sixteen-ounce T-bones," he told the waitress. "What about you, Heinemann?"

"Good God, no," Heinemann laughed. "The New York strip will be more than adequate."

"Excuse the shoptalk, Miss Cove, but what's with Dobbs?" Mac asked Heinemann.

"Christa," she corrected him. "I'm happy to concentrate on the lager."

Heinemann shrugged with some irritation. "He's all upset as usual, asking a million ridiculous questions."

"Isn't the FAA report good enough for him?"

"He says he doesn't believe in coincidences. Two planes in two weeks. He was carrying on about overloading, improper condition . . ."

Mac listened silently.

"Well, was the plane overloaded?" Heinemann finally asked.

Mac was thinking out loud. "It might have carried three or four hundred pounds over restrictions, but this was a still day. That's standard operating, you know that. A plane is graded to carry a certain weight. When there's atmosphere to fight we load it light, on a day like this, we load it heavy. As for the plane, Evert doesn't send them out any way but A-1. But he only checks on what the pilots tell him. He hasn't any crystal ball hooked up to those crates."

"Then that brings it back to pilot error," Heinemann said. "What kind of a pilot is he? How was he checked out?"

Mac grinned wryly. "Those have to be your questions, not Dobbs's. Rick was Dobbs's boy all the way. He came in to me with a letter from Dobbs when Dobbs first came aboard."

Mac looked at Heinemann straight on, waiting for him to think that question through again. "That's a half-assed question, if you forgive my terminology. Of course I checked him out. I looked at his license and I watched him fly. But any half-wit with a slide rule and some folding green can get a license. Add some air time and you have a pilot. A duster is something else. I would never have hired him—too young, too tight-faced. They can fly all right, the younger the better, but they lack judgment."

Heinemann nodded. "Is there a pilot that can take over until Rick's back on his feet? Anyone at all in the wings?"

"What would we do if we had him?" Mac asked. "Evert and I checked out that plane. It's a long way from a crop load. Got somebody in mind?"

"Dobbs has," Heinemann said, suddenly busy with his plate. "Some guy that was out here with him today."

That spooky sense of unease stirred Mac in his seat. "Big, rangy guy with a southern drawl?"

Heinemann looked up, surprised. "Know him?"

"Only by reputation. He's been hanging out with my crew in town."

"That makes sense." Heinemann nodded. "A duster out of work might be nosing in this valley."

"But how come he hooked up to Dobbs?" Mac challenged. "I'm the handy one here in the valley."

Heinemann shrugged. "In any case, Dobbs is pushing for you to take on this guy."

"We haven't any plane for him," Mac said stubbornly.

"Maybe we can solve that too," Heinemann soothed. "Dobbs is pressing this so hard that I promised you'd check this guy out come Saturday. Dobbs will be down to get his P-39 ready for some big show that following day."

"Jesus," Mac groaned. "As tight as my schedule is?"

"It takes a half hour," Heinemann reminded him. "It might cool Dobbs off a little. That's worth something." Heinemann reached across the table for Christa's hand. "Sorry for this shoptalk about people you don't even know."

"I've met Stanley Dobbs before," she told him. "At a friend's party down by Stanford. He's got a lovely wife, really a beautiful girl."

"That explains the way he was staring at you," Heinemann said. "Both at the dock and when we were at the hospital."

"I never actually met him so he's forgiven for not remembering me. In fact, I was more interested in his wife. We had a good talk."

Then suddenly she turned to Mac. "But you I am interested in, Mac. Tell me about dusting."

"You got all night?" Mac laughed.

She chuckled. "It's just so new to me, and scary."

"It's Rick that makes it scary," Heinemann told her. "Most of the time it's just long hours of hard work. Right, Mac?"

"The numbers are scary," Mac disagreed. "All those write-ups you see in the papers about private planes and corporate jets going down, they add up to only about one and a half accidents for every hundred thousand air hours. But dusting, there's four and a fourth dusting deaths for the same air time. Not the best odds going.

"Walter's on the money about long hours of hard work, but those are flying hours. Seeding or dusting or spraying, a man can get more flying in than in any other business."

"Spraying," she mused.

"Poison, fertilizer, seeds, sulfur," Mac recited. "We fight everything, bugs and bacteria and shrimps in the rice."

"They also herd ducks," Heinemann put in.

"And warm up cold trees by stirring the air around them and drop slurry on fires. We get around."

"You'd think you would run out of bugs."

"No chance," Mac replied. "Even with what we do, the crop losses from bugs run to five billion dollars a year. We keep food coming cheap. That's our business."

"Airplanes cheaper than human labor?" Christa laughed. "Now come on."

"It takes a hundred man-hours to raise an acre of rice in the Orient," Heinemann told her. "In California we figure on eight man-hours."

She nodded soberly. "But there's still the danger."

"The fliers take the worst chances," Mac agreed. "Them and the ground crews. Special clothes, respirators with interchangeable filters, rubber boots, and still they have to have checkups to monitor the poison in their systems. It builds up and they have to lay off a while. As for accidents, they generally happen to people outside the business only because they are trespassing . . . or can't read." His glance slid to Heinemann, remembering Donnie Sutter.

She shook her head. "With such toxicity, there ought to be a better way."

"They're on it all the time," Heinemann assured her. "A lot of the research is paying off in these new poisons with limited periods of toxicity. That's why they are so carefully posted. Once exposed to air they start to lose strength or we couldn't use them on foodstuffs like lettuce or fruit."

"You two are a walking college course," Christa said.

"We better stay up on it." Mac laughed. "There are thirty-one agencies looking over my shoulder all the time."

Christa rose at Heinemann's signal, pulling on her sweater. "See, he's trying to get me away before I become an expert on violent death."

With Rick's condition reported as "stable," Mac started back to the strip. A full moon bathed the valley in light. His belly was comfortably tight against the seat belt. Let Dobbs bring his fair-haired Texan out for a joy ride. Heinemann was with him and that was what mattered.

Cramar was on the phone when he heaved himself into the trailer. She covered the mouthpiece to turn to him. Her face was pale and tear-streaked.

"It's the hospital," she whispered. "Rick just took a turn."

He took the phone and listened, mumbling and then nodding as the sickness rose in his chest. The brain surgery had been a success. The internal injuries had gotten him at last.

"You go home," he told Cramar, reaching into his personnel file. "I'll do this with his kin before I do anything else."

When Cramar opened the door to leave, Mac heard a day bird calling mournfully, confused by the brilliance of the moonlight. With something hard resting at the back of his throat he set out a fresh package of Camels and began dialing long distance.

13

Wednesday, May 1

Aside from the help at Mary's Steakhouse and a few scattered ranchers who had met Rick in their fields, the dead pilot had few friends in Blakeslea. Unlike most of the pilots who rented houses and settled into the community, Rick had lived like a transient in one motel after another.

But communities like Blakeslea take violent death seriously, and although the actual funeral would be in Louisiana where Rick came from, Walter Heinemann made arrangements for a memorial service in the local church. Never mind that one day Rick was only one of the dusters from the Flying Mick, the day after the accident he became a man they had seen ("Why it couldn't have been more than a week ago") and now he was dead. To have known a person even by sight created a vicarious intimacy with the victim. Such was the majesty of death that strangers were compelled to huddle together in the shared relief of their own survival.

Walter was delighted when Christa offered to come along. The endless trips had grown tiresome, and alone among women, he had yet to find her company tedious.

Since Wednesday was always the busiest day on his calendar, Walter carefully figured the timing from back to front. The service was scheduled for two. A half-hour drive from the Nut Tree meant they should be at that restaurant at twelve. If he picked Christa up at eleven there would be just enough slack to compensate for the rush of the lunch hour.

Walter realized with satisfaction that only one item on his calendar had not been crossed out.

"Any word from Crane?" he called to Pat through the open office door.

First the clatter of her typewriter ceased and then the hum as she snapped it off. Instead of answering his question, she jumped ahead of his thought and came to the door, her expression subdued.

"I don't mind waiting here until he comes back," she said. "I'm not eating lunch this week anyway."

Walter had been astonished at her reaction to Rick's death. She had never seen the man nor heard his name until this week. Still, when she was making the calls to the florist for a wreath to be sent to Louisiana and to Blakeslea for the details of the service, her usually crisp voice had turned gentle and vulnerable.

"You're looking awfully nice today," Walter said impulsively. "I noticed earlier but got caught up here." She had done something different with her hair. Instead of the loops, she had pulled it straight back and caught it with a ribbon the same shade of pink as her sweater.

She flushed and shook her head unhappily. "My diet is going awfully slow this time," she said, like a confession. "But I'm staying right in there. I am fully committed this time."

She turned away at the sound of the outer door opening, and Walter concealed his smile. Nobody, especially not Pat September, likes to realize their private wars are the source of merriment.

He listened idly to her voice rising and falling in the outer room and glanced at his watch. Jesus. He hoped this would not be a new customer who he would have to fob off because of his schedule. He had spent too much time with Christa and the Flying Mick. He needed to coddle some new accounts into firm contracts.

He heard Pat insisting that he was due for an appointment within minutes and the man's voice promising to be brief. At least she had set the stage for his exit, Walter thought, as he rose to greet the man in his doorway.

The man Pat introduced as Alex Fuller looked to be in his mid-thirties. His clothes disqualified him as a customer. His life style obviously didn't include custom-designed yachts. His coat was a hair too wide in the shoulders for his bones and his trousers revealed a startling half inch of wooly white sock.

But his face was the dangerous kind, so nondescript that Walter could have met him a dozen times without remembering. In deference to that possibility, Walter smiled broadly as he leaned across the desk and offered his hand.

Pressed as he was by the time and the afternoon that lay ahead, Walter did not at once absorb the man's identification. When he did realize who was facing him, a slow coldness started in his gut.

"Excuse me," he said, and went to the door.

When Pat looked up he nodded at her. "If Crane calls while Mr. Fuller is here, have him leave a number." Then he smiled. "I'll just shut this door against your decibel count."

She grinned, wriggling her nose at him, and went back to her steady crashing at the typewriter keys.

In the closed room, the coldness in Alex Fuller's eyes became almost palpable. Once his identification was complete, he handed Walter a small white envelope then nodded briskly and moved to the door.

Only in the open doorway did he speak again.

"Have a nice day," he called back to Walter. The irony in his tone was so delicate that Pat, looking up at him from her desk, missed it completely.

Walter weighed the envelope in his hand. All of his missions had come like this, always a new agent appearing without advance notice. Without exception he had felt excited and exhilarated by the opportunity to perform in this role. This time the envelope itself felt different. He tapped it delicately against his hand before he cleared his desk and picked up his briefcase.

"I'm taking you up on your offer to wait for Crane," he told Pat. "I have an errand to run before I leave. And thanks a lot, Pat. You're a gem." He paused and forced a smile. "Have a nice hungry afternoon!"

She groaned as he closed the door.

In his apartment, Walter draped his jacket across the back of a chair. A late morning breeze fanned the drapes at the window as he opened the envelope.

The orders had never been this brief. The decoding took only a few minutes and then he checked the words again, incredulous at that first reading.

It was then that he poured himself a stiff double shot of Haig and Haig.

STANLEY DOBBS EXTREMELY DANGEROUS. HE REPRESENTS PERILOUS THREAT TO YOUR MISSION. MEANS OF DEATH YOUR OWN DECISION. MISSION MUST BE COMPLETED WITHIN TEN DAYS.

The Scotch didn't touch the cold impact of the words. Stanley Dobbs. God in heaven. He watched the thin paper in the ashtray blacken and curl. He crushed the frail remains in a Kleenex before shaking the ashes of charred paper over his deck rail. They floated weightless through the branches of the eucalyptus on the slope below.

Murder. No, not murder but execution. The end was the same. A tremor of excitement stirred. His designer's mind began to sort the possibilities. He turned to the gold-framed calendar on his mantle. Ten days.

But there was fear, too. There was always a margin for error in the most immaculate design. He had considered the risks with the other assignments. Was he reacting differently because of death or Christa?

He caught himself staring blindly at the calendar and shook himself briskly. There was nothing he could do this day or this hour. He bolted the windows shut and closed the drapes against the coming sun of afternoon. When he returned from Rick's memorial service he could begin to plan.

It was a few minutes before two that Wednesday as Stanley Dobbs eased his car into one of the few remaining parking places on Willow Avenue in Blakeslea. As he walked toward the First Baptist Church he passed Walter Heinemann's gleaming silver Porsche parked between two pickup trucks. One of the trucks was full of chicken crates. A limp mound of feed sacks piled on them gave off an odor of hot dust as he passed.

The square white church promised to be a hot box. Its leaded windows were closed against the sun that blazed through the meager foliage of a live oak tree whose branches were festooned with web worms. From inside Dobbs heard the hushed murmur of voices. The smell of chrysanthemums hung in the air. Somewhere near the front of the church, hidden by the bare wooden pulpit, a fan was whirring, its slow racketing rhythm providing a background for the whispering tenants of the pews. Heinemann was already there with that Cove girl, Christen, no Christa.

Not until he was directly alongside did Dobbs realize that the broad man with the pasted-down hair and the ill-fitting blue suit was Mac Maguire. He had never seen Mac in anything but a jumpsuit. He looked helpless, like a water creature turned out onto land.

With the stiff greeting past, Dobbs retreated to a curved pew where the fan's noisy labor produced a vague movement of air around his ankles. He looked around the church curiously. He'd never been in one of these. It was as different from the Russian Orthodox churches of his boyhood as it was from the darkly formal Episcopal church that Ginger supported with her money and her good works.

It wasn't easy for him to remember exactly how his own church looked anymore. He had a blurred memory of the stations framed in reddish wood, the figures squat and short-legged like the characters in the Brueghel prints that Ginger's decorator had chosen for the game room.

The church was completely filled within a few minutes of his arrival. He recognized the rancher he and Jackson had called on. The wife's cinnamon hair looked darker in this light. Her shirtwaist dress, the belt pinned into place, flared over her ample hips. She looked as if her feet hurt.

The three young girls took longer to figure out. The tear-stained one in the middle was the prettiest, a thin girl with half-developed breasts and a teased hair style that shrunk her small pointed face. Every once in a while she dabbed at her eyes with a ball of handkerchief. She must have been Rick's girl. Her friend cradled her elbow in a solicitous hand. She had to be twenty-one, Dobbs realized, having seen her balancing trays of beer at Mary's Steakhouse.

The round-faced minister almost disappeared behind the masses of wreaths as he mounted the pulpit. The room shuffled into a stillness that was only broken by the hum of a plane making a pass above a nearby field. At the sound a muffled sob came from the back of the church where the thin girl crouched between her friends.

Dobbs's attention strayed as the minister's voice droned in that monotone that was apparently issued to these men with their long dark robes. Mac seemed burdened by his own hands. He alternately nodded, as if in prayer, and stared vacantly at the round stained-glass window above the minister's head. The bastard was probably Roman, Dobbs thought. He missed the white choker and the Greek retreat of his faith.

When Toby had died, Dobbs had been in Denver at a meeting. He had sent flowers, of course, but was spared that ordeal. He glanced at Heinemann, whose handsome secret face was turned straight ahead. The Cove girl at his side was far and away the coolest thing in the sweltering room. Dobbs studied the upward tilt of her nose, the faint, almost silvery aura of light on her fair hair. Sensing his eyes on her she turned slightly so that the startling green of her eyes met his full on. Maybe he imagined the warmth in her expression as she nodded before turning her eyes away.

At least this would be the end of Mac. It couldn't work out any other way. The shop was short a plane as well as a pilot. He would buy the damned plane himself and put Jackson up in it if it had to be that way. But Mac had to go.

Dobbs had checked quietly and thoroughly. No one had seen Mac take up a plane since he got back from burying Toby. Thelma Cramar, defensive as always, had been truculent about his question. "When would he have time to play around with flying as busy as he is?"

It was all over with Mac. Jackson was as good as into that chief pilot slot. Then he could start running the shop his own way.

An older woman, her back stained with moisture, pumped the organ through the final hymn. The strains of the music softened to a whisper as the minister passed down the aisle to post himself at the door.

Beyond in the street Dobbs saw a flash of red. A police car, motor running, blocked the lane as two uniformed officers in shirt sleeves moved toward the crowd of demonstrators. Over the dying strains of the organ and the minister's lugubrious voice came shouts and other sirens in the distance.

Once free of the church, Dobbs watched the demonstrators retreat rebelliously. Mostly they were very young, but one older man stayed to argue with the police. The only word Dobbs could hear was *Rights*. Always it was rights, Dobbs thought wearily. A tall girl with a body like Eloise's was holding up a sign that read "ONE LESS POISONER OF OUR CHILDREN."

The signs were pretty effective for a hick rally, he decided, and a television cameraman was hopping across the lawns getting it all soaked up. BABY KILLERS, LIVE BY THE (skull and crossbones), DIE BY THE (skull and crossbones). Pretty effective copy.

Dobbs waited for Heinemann as the demonstrators were backed off the street to stand staring angrily at anyone who met their eyes. The sheriff's car stayed too, its red light blazing steadily into the paler sunlight.

"We need to talk," he told Heinemann, nodding briefly to Christa.

"Now?" Heinemann asked as if in disbelief. The withdrawal in the man's eyes startled Dobbs. Jesus. If the kraut turned hostile on him, he could give twice the fight that Mac had.

"Not this very minute," Dobbs soothed. "But very soon. Over the weekend perhaps."

Heinemann waited impatiently, flipping his car keys in his hand. What in hell had gotten into the bastard?

"I'm taking my plane down south for an air show Sunday," Dobbs reminded him. "I have Saturday free. Would that be all right with you?"

Heinemann exchanged a glance with Christa before replying.

"Saturday is all right. What time?" Again his voice was coldly civil.

"I have to spend the night out here to take my plane out early enough," Dobbs explained. "If we could make it Saturday afternoon, say about two? I mean to bring Jackson along, the pilot I told you about."

Heinemann shrugged. "Saturday at two then," he said, turning away with Christa's hand caught under his arm.

Dobbs watched the Porsche pull out and turned his mind to

his trip home. He was lucky the thing had gotten over fast. With any luck he could be back at the bank before the afternoon commuter traffic started south from San Francisco.

The man must have been waiting near where Dobbs was parked. Dobbs had his key in the door before he noticed him.

"Mr. Dobbs?" he said, like a question. He didn't look like a rancher, but he was young, maybe thirty. He couldn't be one of the demonstrators. His hair was too short and he was wearing a tie.

"I'm Dobbs," he replied, his tone brusque to discourage the fellow wasting his time.

"I have something for you," the man said quietly. Dobbs's mild annoyance turned to curiosity as the man's steady eyes held his own. Then that tingle of excitement came along with a grudging admiration. Jesus. How cool could a man get? Dobbs found himself tempted to glance around as the man continued to identify himself. Out here in the middle of the day with the church crowd still bumbling around, this son of a bitch was calmly identifying himself as a contact.

"Very well," Dobbs said, his voice a little high. He felt cordial now and excited.

"Please get into your car and roll down the window on this side," the man directed. A rancher and his wife passed the car in easy conversation. The man, now leaning against the door, shifted his position and nodded at them as they passed.

Then he leaned into the window, smiling as he offered his hand to Dobbs for a handshake. "Have a safe trip home," he said as he backed away. Only with the tail of his eye had Dobbs caught the flash of white as the envelope slid from the man's hand to be hidden between the passenger seat and the door. Dobbs made no move to retrieve it. Instead, he waved at the man and pulled away from the curb, his heart pounding.

A few miles west of Blakeslea on the county road was a widened shoulder baked dry by the valley sun. Dobbs had seen truckers sleeping there in their rigs and campers picnicking in the shade of the rough trees that rose from the field beyond. Dobbs drove to the spot and pulled off.

He sat a moment quietly before loosening his tie and removing his coat. He hung it on the monogrammed hangar that Ginger had ordered from a shop in Maiden Lane. With the envelope in his hand he looked up and down the deserted stretch of road. He took his flask from the glove compartment and took a deep scorching draft of Jack Daniels. He could feel it clearing his head of the scent of funeral flowers and the dust of the town.

When he pulled his lips from the flask it felt light. He held it against the light, shrugged and finished it off before replacing it in the glove compartment.

The deciphering went slowly because first he had to recall the code. But there was no way he had the patience to wait until he got home.

When he finally had it, written in scrawling letters across the back of the envelope, he whistled softly.

"Walter Heinemann extremely dangerous," he had written. "He represents perilous threat to your mission. Means of death your own decision. Mission must be completed within ten days."

Dobbs sat stunned a long time after he destroyed the envelope. In his rearview mirror he saw a state patrol car on the road from town. He fished a map from his side pocket. As the patrolman slowed, Dobbs held up the opened map and made a circle with his fingers to show that he was all right. When the patrol car became only a spot in the distance, Dobbs eased back onto the road and started for home.

Why in hell had he finished off that whiskey? He could sure use a drink now.

Any other time his curiosity about the mission would have been giving him fits. This was different. This was like an omen. Jesus, this would clean out the shop at a single swoop. First Mac, then Heinemann. It was a sign. He had never missed before when the signs were right. He saw the line of skulls across Eloise's bed. By God the kid had been right after all. With this coming, it was natural enough for her to read all that death. A sign, by God.

14

Wednesday, May 1

As Stanley Dobbs turned into the circle drive that led to his house he glimpsed a flash of color in the grove that lined the road. He slowed as Gretchen, pursued by her dog, emerged from the trees at a dead run. With her long hair flying and her mouth in that wide grin, she challenged him to race the rest of the way to the garage. Before he could touch the accelerator she and the German shorthair were off, long legs pumping across the green, the dog's tongue swaying from side to side and dripping with exertion.

Nobody won. Nobody ever won. As always they reached the garage door at the same second. Gretchen tugged open the door and hopped in beside him leaving the dog to whine pitifully above the puddle of saliva between his front feet.

"You're early," she panted, her breasts rising and falling from her run. "I'm glad."

Dobbs loosened his tie and looked at her. Her legs were scarred from soccer. Her hip-hugger shorts barely covered her small tight bottom and made no attempt to cover the roundness of her smooth belly. The kerchief blouse tied between her breasts only accented their fullness.

"That's why you're not dressed for dinner I guess," he said, grinning at her.

She wrinkled her face. "Don't you start on me. Everyone has been cross here all day.

"And dull," she added. "Lafe has been wrapped in some stupid book and Mom and Aunt Iris . . ." She pulled her mouth down.

"Dull, too?" he said, pulling his jacket off the hangar.

"As dishwater," she said firmly. "I'll beat you at Ping-Pong. I'll even give you a ten-point handicap as a personal favor."

"After a while maybe," he told her. "I need to wind down a little bit."

Then she remembered. Her body seemed to shrink there beside him in the seat. "That's right," she said. "That guy they buried."

"I'm not sure about the burying," he said. "That was really a memorial service we had in the valley."

"I saw it on a news break," she told him.

"There wasn't much to it. Some music and a sermon attended mostly by the men from the area that he flew for. And some people from the company of course."

"Not everyone from the company?"

He shook his head. "This is the busiest season."

"That really good-looking guy, was he there?" She bit her lips to remember. "Walter something."

"He was there," Dobbs told her.

"And the kids with the signs," she reminded him. "And the cops."

"A memorial service is no place for acts like that," he told her.

"There were demonstrators out there last week too," she told him. "When the kid was poisoned."

He looked at her thoughtfully. "I'd forgotten," he admitted.

She was frowning now, stretching those long legs and staring into the darkness around her feet. "Lots of my friends are really into ecology. They get together and make signs like that. And march."

Dobbs waited out her silence.

"I never tell anybody about you, what you do out there. I wouldn't know how to explain it to them."

He sighed and opened his car door. "There are a dozen ways to put it and all of them would be correct and most of them would start a riot. We fertilize nonorganically. We poison insects and plant diseases with substances that are deadly to people. We use up natural resources, gas and metal in those planes. How would they react to that?" His tone was ironic.

She got out and came around to stand by him, folding his jacket over her arm. "I'm not fighting you, Dad. I'm just trying to figure out why you do it. I hear the horror stories, of workers that breathe the dust and get sick, of people poisoned on fruit and the pilots going down like this one today. Is it worth it?"

"Do your friends ever talk about birth control, Gretch? Do they worry about that?"

"Oh gosh yes. Nobody's going to have kids. We're all going to adopt ethnic, you know, Vietnamese, black."

He smiled in spite of himself. "That's part of the same package. People have to eat. The biggest cause of death in this world is starvation. Too many people, not enough food. Nobody wants dead fish and birds on the beach or a sky full of smog. But man can't live on clean water and pure air alone; he also needs food. The war is against starvation and some people get caught in the crossfire. I sure as hell didn't mean to give a lecture. I'm sorry."

She leaned over and nuzzled his face. She smelled of fresh

air and dog. "That was lousy timing," she admitted. "A girl ought to know better."

He grinned, hugging her round skull against his shoulder. "Ping-Pong if I get unwound in time, okay?"

Lafe's presence in the house was apparent from the thump of recorded music from the bedroom wing. In the dining room fresh poppies were reflected in the polished teak of the table, gleaming wine glasses and napkins were in place.

"Ginger, I'm home," he called.

She was wearing a floor-length orange caftan, slit to the knee to bare slender brown legs. Her arms were cool to his touch.

"Rough, huh?" she asked gently.

He held her a moment. "At least semirough," he agreed.

"Dinner's not until seven-thirty," she said. "You have lots of time."

Dobbs purposefully kept his mind clear of the mission until he was out of the shower and dressed again. Even with a fresh glass of bourbon he sat a long time at his desk staring unseeing at the matched line of pictures behind the lamp.

Walter Heinemann dangerous? It was fruitless to challenge the statement, but its cause caught at his mind. How could he be dangerous, a man who mollycoddled that stupid Mac? Whose soft-voiced machinations had made him every man's favorite politician? Come on. Maybe that hand-tailored facade hid a man he didn't know. German. Ex-Nazis were turning up everywhere. CIA?

It was fruitless to speculate. Walter Heinemann was to die.

The chair was confining. He paced the room, which was beginning to be permeated with the scent of cooking food, a mingled odor of wine and onions and beef. The house was quickening toward evening. His own exhilaration came and went. This offered a greater risk than he had faced before. But opportunity is the harvest of risk taking. His instinct had been right about the Flying Mick. The earlier missions had been only tests. If this was a test and he had the company under his control, there was no way but up.

He read his copy of the Flying Mick partnership agreement through carefully. The contract had been a bear to write. On the death of a partner an assessment would be made of the actual value of the company. The original investment of the deceased member would be transferred to the estate of the deceased along with a percentage of growth reflected by the difference in actual value between time of purchase and time of death. Tandem insurance policies, made payable to the surviving partners, insured that capital resources would be available to meet this obligation without liquidating any assets.

There would be just himself and Mac after Heinemann was dead.

The important thing was to keep himself clean. He thought of Jackson and realized that Jackson was a man who could kill.

Silence was the most expensive commodity that money could buy.

He had to do it himself. He had ten days to figure out a surefire way. The fact that Walter lived alone (give or take an overnight broad) would make it easier. The guy also fished and sailed alone. He thought of Walter's boat, a racing sloop with crisp clear lines and a motor assist. An explosion in the right part of a boat with stored gasoline was a thought.

No matter how Heinemann died, he would be among the suspects because of their joint business venture and that partnership agreement. The thing was to be sure that he didn't miss the first time.

As a college student he had hunted. He remembered the marrow-deep cold of Michigan woods in winter, frozen clouds of breath and the suddenness of gunfire startling blood onto snow. He was no trap-setter. He was a hunter and killer.

The gun was no problem. He had a small revolver with a silencer, found after an abortive robbery attempt at the bank some years before. And Walter lived alone.

He tried to picture it. At three in the morning the doorbell rings. Even if he has a broad he sure as hell wouldn't send her to the door at that hour. That split second at the door, the gun pressed into that supercilious face Gretchen thought handsome. Over and out.

Even the night was set up. His reservation was confirmed at the motel just north of Blakeslea the night before the air show. The trip to Sausalito could be made after he was known to be in bed. A ring on the bell of Walter's apartment, the shot in the face, and the familiar ride back to the valley before dawn.

"You missed your chance to get skunked at Ping-Pong," Gretchen called from outside the door. "Dinner is ready."

The candlelight was reflected on the glass doors that led to the pool; they caught and diffused again on its smooth surface. For a confused moment, Stanley Dobbs saw fire everywhere, a myriad of dancing points of light leading into the darkness of the trees.

He drew his hand over his eyes, frowning.

"At least it's over," Ginger said quietly as he held her chair for her.

Her Aunt Iris looked at him with sympathy. "First the accident, then that poor child and now the pilot. It must be over because it is the third one."

Lafe corrected her, his dark eyes solemn on her face. "The accident doesn't count. It is only death that comes in threes."

Dobbs looked at him but the boy was already a million miles away, jabbing at his food as if he hadn't spoken at all.

"Out of the mouths of babes," Dobbs thought wryly, still staring at the crown of his son's head. For that swift second he saw those tarot cards of Eloise's again, the boy, Rick, and then Walter Heinemann.

No wonder the freaky girl had been scared off.

15

May 1

Walter Heinemann saw Stanley Dobbs's face in the rearview mirror of his Porsche as he pulled from the curb. He cursed himself silently. He had been too blunt, too negative. With luck Dobbs might conclude his brusqueness was due to the service just past, but it was unlikely. The next few days demanded extreme caution. If he had to set a trap for Dobbs, Dobbs must not suspect anything.

A maxim from his childhood in the green woods of Vilna came back to him.

"The tooth of a trap is surprise."

He turned to see Christa frowning beside him.

"Ready to start back?" he asked.

She sighed.

"Have a better idea?" he asked, intrigued by her expression.

"Mac," she said quietly. "He looks so gray and beaten."

"I told you about his son, Toby," he reminded her.

She nodded and laid her hand on his arm. "Let's just go out and stay with him a while. He needs you, you know."

She was right of course. In a miserable green vinyl chair that Mac dragged in from the lounge, Walter watched Christa bring life back into Mac's face. It wasn't anything she said as much as the way she led Mac's thinking. Her eyes were always eager when Mac swiveled in his chair to speak to her. There was a quality to her listening that brought words spinning from Mac's tongue to their mutual delight. As they talked, Walter idly studied Mac's work area, the papers stacked to the bottom row of the key rack where that yellow tagged key held a central place. Jackets were piled high on the coat rack and the color of the desk under those stacks of paper was anybody's guess. Yet when Thelma Cramar called from the other room, Mac instantly located the specific paper she needed.

Strange, untidy savage, Walter thought affectionately. Not a hair of malice on his head. Dobbs. He rose suddenly.

"Good God, Christa, it will be night before we get home."

Mac glanced at the clock and groaned. "And I'll be until morning shoveling this stuff." Then he grinned, his eyes twinkling. "You're what I call a major distraction, Christa Cove."

"I'll take that for what it is," Christa said, smiling. "Pure Irish blarney."

Once they were free of the traffic, Walter laid his hand on Christa's knee. "I've figured out what kind of a scientist you are," he announced with triumph.

"Oh?" she asked, her eyes challenging him.

"Animal behaviorist," he announced. "Practice limited to primates only."

Her laugh sounded almost relieved.

Walter parked the Porsche in Christa's carport and sat listening to the neighborhood sounds. Although the sun still blazed on the other side of Mount Tamalpais, it felt like twilight, twilight with the day draining away. Faint strains of rock music came from the hill above, a snatch of laughter began, only to be drowned by the imperative barking of a dog. Someone had thrown hickory chips onto charcoal. The fragrance mingled with the richness of burning beef fat. Although he and Christa had stopped for dinner on the way down, the smoke from the grill still smelled appealing, suggesting conviviality and the careless informality of family and friends.

In the dusk, the bones of her face were glossed with an inner light and her hair reflected the remarkable color of her eyes. Her tailored suit was immaculately fitted and the explosion of white stock tie at her throat had added just the right note at the memorial service in Blakeslea. It wasn't normal the way she managed to do everything right. But then he was smarting again about his incivility to Dobbs. As hard-driving as Dobbs had been in his behavior toward Mac, the man was not insensitive. It had been careless and dangerous to behave like that when so much rested on retaining normalcy.

Christa had worn her hair up all day, revealing a distracting curve of smooth untanned neck. Now she released it into a silken mass around her shoulders, partially concealing her face.

"Thank the little lady for coming out today," Mac had whispered as Walter left. "She was a cool wind."

Strange poetical Irish. "A cool wind."

"Where would you like to go, Christa?" he asked suddenly.

She frowned at him, her eyes solemn.

"This is a game," he told her. "If you had nothing to do, no plans at all, where would you like to go?"

She pressed her lips together. When she began to speak, her tone was monotonous as if she was describing something printed inside her closed eyelids.

"There is sun, sun so hot that the air above the sand is curved with waves of rising heat. Square white buildings are piled against dark cliffs like toy blocks thrown by children."

When he laughed, she held up a cautioning hand.

"I haven't finished. There are small round tables under colored umbrellas and even with your windows closed you can hear the crash of the surf."

"That's all?"

She turned and smiled at him. "There's you and me, of course," she added as if his question had been ridiculous. "And chocolates in fluted paper cups when we wake up after love-making."

"And where is this sun?" he asked. "The Bahamas?"

She shook her head. "I have an unreasonable fear of falling coconuts."

"The Riviera perhaps?"

She raised one eyebrow in amazement. "And watch you wear your eyes out ogling French beauties?"

"Not if you were there," he assured her.

"It is a rule with me never to trust a man whose lip trembles like that when he pronounces 'Riviera.' " She echoed his accent so precisely that he exploded into laughter.

"Baja," he decided aloud. "It's near enough that we could fly there."

"It's a date," she said, snuggling down in her seat.

"I'll hold you to that," Walter said firmly. "In fact, we leave very early Saturday."

She stared at him reproachfully. "I thought you said this was a game."

"So I changed my mind."

"I will have to be going home."

"When?" he asked.

"Soon," she said quietly. "Within the week."

"But I'm not tired of us yet," he protested. "You didn't warn me."

She laughed. "How gallant of you. Have you decided when this boredom will set in? What if I said two more weeks, or a month?"

He reached for her in the bucket seat and caught her awkwardly, struggling to find her face in that mass of hair.

"Let's go back to my place," he whispered against her neck. His hand found the smooth satin of her inner thigh as he spoke.

"Not tonight," she said, pressing his hand away.

"What's the matter with tonight?"

"You are tired," she told him. "Something has lain behind your eyes all day."

"Then I need sleep."

She nodded. "Sleep alone."

"Tomorrow then?" he asked. "What time tomorrow?"

Her eyes were level on his. "Whenever you are through with what's hanging in your head. I want all of your attention," she teased.

"I may call you at dawn," he warned.

"I might even answer," she replied after lifting her mouth to his.

All the way home he kept toying with the thought of just the two of them with sun and sea for a day, a week, however long it took for his passion for her to subside. It was appealing, damned appealing.

But this was the kind of involvement he had ruled out of his life as being extraneous, even dangerous. How could the most discreet man conceal a clandestine second life from a woman he was genuinely involved with? Impossible. Look at how quickly she had sensed his distraction with the new mission. "Something behind your eyes."

Once at home he stripped and showered. The smell of poison from the Flying Mick had stayed in his head all the way home. It hung in his clothes and his hair. Still undressed, he stretched across the bed with the TV chattering from across the room.

It was no good. He was restless in that room without her. And there was this business to be done. With so little time.

He filled a tumbler of Scotch, frowning at his own generosity, and pulled a director's chair out onto the deck.

The sun was wholly gone, leaving the sky still pale from day. Beyond the wooded hump of Belvedere and the staggered lights of Tiburon, Berkeley and Oakland twinkled unsteadily in the cooling air. Above the vague silhouette of the hills behind them rose a starless immensity of sky. Where stars should have been, the lights of a 707 turned and wheeled on approach to Oakland International.

Stanley Dobbs was his enemy. He forced his mind from the inevitable questions. It wasn't his responsibility to know why this remarkable judgment had been made. The man who had been his partner was now his enemy.... "Dangerous to your mission ..." the directive had stated. Dobbs must die.

The quick way to death was through a gun. A gun involved proximity. There was always the tedious exploration of the victim's last acts, the miracle of modern scientific investigation that could damn a man from a distant laboratory. And the physical problem of the weapon itself, obtaining it, disposing of it. Guns were untidy.

He must not be hurried at this stage, he warned himself. The planning was the most important part of any mission. His acts must be as immaculately detailed as the blueprints on his drawing boards; no angle could be misjudged.

But planning was his forte. At least he was on firm ground here.

His Scotch glass was mysteriously empty. With a rueful foreknowledge of the price he would pay in the morning, he refilled the glass and propped his bare feet on the railing. The sky had darkened enough to make low stars visible.

What did he really know of Stanley Dobbs, his life, his schedule, his weaknesses (aside from a frustrating inability to let well enough alone at the Flying Mick)?

Walter replayed his partner in his mind. He seemed an exemplary husband. He could be an almost fatuous parent when he talked of his daughter, Gretchen. His reputation in the banking community was above reproach. Only a man with courage that approached foolhardiness would fly that wild plane of his. Although he drank socially, he apparently never let this taste get out of hand.

Walter glanced guiltily at his own nearly empty glass.

Somewhere in the mixed bag that was Stanley Dobbs was a flaw that Walter must find, a flaw that could be exploited secretly and lethally.

But not tonight. He carefully maneuvered the chair back through the glass doors and into its place. He sank, nude and chilled, across the bed thinking of Christa in sunlight.

Tomorrow, he told himself. An inspiration would come tomorrow.

By ten-seventeen that next morning Walter had finished the first pot of coffee. Pat September started a second one with a grumble.

"That's all we need around here," she told him acidly. "A set of caffeine jangles on top of Crane's hysteria and your deadline on that yawl."

By eleven-thirty he had finished the last sketch on the yawl and left it with the draftsman to dress up for the presentation. He was checking his calendar for his next obligation when the inspiration came.

At ten minutes to twelve, he left for the library.

"When will you be back?" Pat asked as he spun past her desk.

He seemed remarkably jovial as he turned to wave at her.

"Whenever you see me, baby, whenever you see me."

She slammed the ON button of her typewriter and poised her hands above the irregular hum. She was hungry. Men weren't worth it, they really weren't worth it at all.

16

Blakeslea, California, Friday, May 3

The Friday morning traffic was heavy as Walter Heinemann worked his way onto Highway 80. At least the traffic wasn't bothering Christa. She was curled comfortably beside him with her eyes closed.

"You probably should have stayed home and sacked in," he teased her.

One yellow eye opened defiantly. "I'm not sleeping, I'm only resting."

He laughed. "Then rest for both of us. My head is still full of last night. And my stomach, too," he added ruefully. "And we have to figure on an early start tomorrow."

She wriggled her shoulders before falling to sleep again. That had been the night, he smiled to himself. Once he had researched and tested the last immaculate detail of his plan to eliminate Stanley Dobbs, a curious peace had settled over him, much as if the mission was already completed.

He had even been lucky enough to find Stanley Dobbs at his desk and have him free for Walter's own convenience. He had felt a kind of childish pride at how easy Dobbs had been to handle.

"I don't know what was on my mind when I agreed to meet you and your pilot friend at the field Saturday," he told Dobbs. "I guess I was not myself because of that service and those crazy kids with their signs."

"You can't make it then?" Dobbs clearly sounded disappointed. "It's damned important to the company."

"I couldn't agree with you more," Walter had told him. "Would Friday be possible, say Friday afternoon? I have to leave town Saturday morning, but if you and the fellow could be there Friday . . ."

"No problem," Dobbs had replied, genial with relief. "Say between noon and two?"

"Perfect," Walter agreed. "And, Stan, thanks a lot for being so obliging. This trip just came up . . ."

"No sweat," Dobbs assured him. "See you tomorrow then."

With that done he could call Christa and announce he was "through."

"Your entire attention," she insisted.

"You are about to receive a lesson in attention," he warned her.

They had eaten at Ondine's, a dinner that would cost him a painful penance in the exercise room. After changing, they had taken the boat to Angel Island Cove for the night.

The moon had risen over the Berkeley Hills, as thin as a wafer and larger than Walter ever remembered. Its reflection broke into pleated bands of light as the boat fretted at anchor. The breakfast they cooked on the beach left them scarce enough time to sail home and dress for this trip to the valley. Christa had so blandly assumed that she would go to the Flying Mick with him that he hadn't the heart to protest. My God, any other woman would be racing around buying things and making arrangements to leave the following morning for Baja. Not Christa. Instead she stirred a little in her sleep beside him.

And indeed, having her there helped distract him from his endless rehearsal of the trap he would set for Stanley Dobbs. It kept his mind from veering into the doubts that came whenever he considered the consequences of his plan for the coming afternoon.

As a man who had made a legion of designs only to find small errors too late, he was wary of the simplicity of his scheme. There must be a hidden margin for error that he had not predicted. The individual steps he must make had been painfully practiced in his mind. He needed only to get Mac out of that office for a split second and then to have . . . at the most . . . three to five minutes in the second hangar alone.

The time alone in the hangar might be a problem. He would have to fob Christa off during the time he set the death trap. He could feel the necessary tools inside the pocket of his sailing jacket. The weight of the plastic bag was reassuring: wire cutters (in case he was wrong about the key), the surgical gloves, a slender chemical vial, and a key marked with yellow.

As Walter turned onto the valley road, Christa wakened and stretched luxuriously. "Now I am rested, how about you?"

"Thanks a lot," he laughed. "I'm even prepared to take on an argument with the redoubtable Dobbs."

She looked at him, puzzled. "Tense maybe, but I don't see him that way. Is that why we came, for an argument?"

"That's my guess," Walter said. "From what he said at the service Wednesday I gather he's bringing some hotshot pilot out here with a view to getting us to hire him as Rick's replacement."

"And you don't want to?"

"It makes no sense and Dobbs knows it. Mac and I gave him all the numbers on it. We need both a man and a plane, which are cheaper to hire as a package than separately. If we hire someone, we have to buy a plane we won't need when Rick's plane is back on the line. Except in rice season we already have extra planes; we even rent them out to areas with different crop patterns off season. The only reason I came was to settle Dobbs down before we leave for our sun and sand."

"Tomorrow," she sighed, tightening her arms around herself. "Tomorrow, sun and sand and surf."

"That's an early flight," he reminded her. "You better be packed."

"So how long does it take to fold a bikini?" she asked.

"You weren't serious about leaving next week, were you?"

She laid her hand on his leg. "Don't push," she said softly. "A day at a time works best."

A day at a time. She was right, of course. This day he would set his trap for Dobbs. Tomorrow they would leave for Baja at dawn. When Dobbs died on Sunday they would send for him and interrupt his Mexican vacation. Too bad. But he would be too far away, so physically removed from any suspicion of complicity that he could return only grieving and shocked.

They had given him ten days. A surge of pride rose at the cleverness of his trap and how swiftly it would be sprung.

By the time they arrived at the Flying Mick, the muscles along Walter's back ached from tension. He relaxed them consciously. He was winding up too tight. Nothing could go wrong. After a leisurely lunch, they had still arrived little after one. Three, five minutes at the most, were all he needed unless he had to cut wires. As he eased into the lot the dogs set up their howling beyond their fence.

"This is the place." Christa grinned, laying her hands over her ears.

The scent of the chemicals on the heavy afternoon air filled Walter's head, starting a rhythm like nausea at the back of his throat. "The right smell too," he said, his words lost in the roaring of a Stearman that taxied down the strip as he spoke.

From this point every moment was vital. He cupped Christa's elbow in his hand and hailed the mechanic loading a truck.

"Where's Mac?" he shouted.

When the man waved toward Evert's machine shop, Walter

felt a small flutter of relief. That was one problem solved. He had only needed to get Mac out of the office briefly. Having him already out was a bonus he hadn't dreamed of. The position of Cramar's desk in relation to Mac's made her no threat at all.

As he walked with Christa past the hangars to the machine shop Walter felt the countdown begin in his belly. It was as if a silent metronome had begun to sway away the precious seconds that must be utilized to the last beat. Yet he must appear unhurried. Every movement must be relaxed and unhurried.

Passing the hangar where Dobbs's Aircobra was stored, Walter saw with relief that the door was unlocked. In fact, the door stood a little ajar as if to air out the place. The other hangar where the fancy Stearman shared space with the storage area for restricted materials was open too, but not all the way. There was only enough space so that a man could enter and leave without needing an extra hand for the door.

Evert glanced up as they entered, stopping only to touch his hat to Christa before resuming his work.

Mac grinned broadly, taking Christa's hands in his. "Good to see you both," he told them. "I expect Dobbs in maybe a half hour."

"I didn't want to be late," Walter said. "Don't let us interrupt what you're doing. We thought we might check out the coffee supply."

Mac nodded. "Good idea. I'll be right along. I told Cramar to start a new brew." He grinned. "If there's a good pot you can see how much weight I carry around here."

"We'll check that out." Walter laughed.

Walter measured his steps as he walked Christa back to the trailer. Steady, he told himself. Steady on.

Once inside he leaned against the wall while Christa and Cramar exchanged their greetings. A faint tingling began along his calves at this feigned relaxation while his mind was screaming for action.

Christa handed him coffee in the heavy blue and white mug that Mac had given to him when they first became partners. "It's like having your shoes under a bed," Mac had explained. "You belong where your mug hangs, right?"

Walter lifted it to his lips only to remove it with a soft whistle.

"You do brew one blazing cup of coffee," he told Cramar, touching his lips tentatively with one finger.

"That's nothing to the heat those men would give me if it wasn't hot enough," she replied. "But I'm with you. My mouth isn't asbestos-lined either."

Setting the cup down deliberately, Walter walked toward Mac's desk. "I'll just take a cup of this out to Mac while mine is cooling down."

As he turned, he shielded Cramar's view of the desk. The substitute key was already in his palm as he turned. He switched keys on the board with his right hand as he lifted Mac's mug from the pile of papers with his left. He turned back, smiling. "We could make him drink what's left in here?"

"You out to poison the guy?" Cramar teased as she turned to rinse the mug.

She looked straight into Walter's eyes as she handed him Mac's filled cup. Her gaze was open and cordial. She had seen nothing. The first hard step had been taken. A tremor of excitement made him slosh the hot coffee over his hand.

With irritating slowness Cramar got a paper napkin and wrapped it around the mug handle. "Hurry for God's sake," he wanted to shriek at her. Instead he nodded his thanks.

Without even glancing at the hangars, Walter carried the coffee directly to Mac in the machine room. "I brought you coffee," he explained. "To brace you for the arrival of our friend."

Evert's eyes moved from Walter to Mac, but he said nothing.

Steeling his pace to a leisurely walk Walter retraced his steps toward the trailer. He walked past the open door of the hangar and then stopped, as if distracted. After the briefest of pauses, and without looking around, he entered the hangar.

Once inside the hangar he froze. The margin for error that he had failed to predict was here and now. It was sound. The noise level of the field was suddenly overwhelming. The throb of a plane motor, the whine from Evert's shop, the steady racket of words and clatter from the crew working among the trucks. My God, he was totally vulnerable to any passing intruder. A man on a horse could come on him without warning in that melee. But to close the door behind him would be hopelessly conspicuous.

He shrugged. It was a gamble, that was all. He moved swiftly past the sharply painted Stearman, concentrating on the labels of the containers within the enclosure.

The storage area was a giant pen built of heavy link fencing about seven feet high. The signs on the gate and the walls of the pen, required by law to be readable from twenty-five feet, were in a bright red that glowed in the slightly darkened hangar. Between the skull and crossbones, the giant word DANGER leaped at Walter as he leaned to try the key in the lock. He had gambled on the key. The clippers were for emergency, but he had taken a chance that the key with the yellow tag on Mac's board fit this pen.

To a duster, yellow is the color of contamination and danger. He had gambled on that.

With a soft click, the key turned and the gate sagged against Walter's knee. He felt his lungs empty with relief. The second hard step.

Walter worked rapidly, forcing his moist right hand into the surgical glove. He passed over the containers marked WARNING or CAUTION, concentrating on those with the word DANGER and the required skull-and-crossbones symbol. The parathion he was seeking, like the others, had a clearly marked label listing not only its name and ingredients but also directions and a registration number.

Tightening his breath against the fumes, Walter eased off the top of the container and filled the glass vial with the poison.

The vial felt cold through the filament of rubber that protected his hand. He thought of the agricultural worker who had inadvertently thrust his hand into a container of this chemical and died the following day.

Catching the rolled wristband of the glove in his left hand, he forced the glove inside out so that the rubber of the glove tightly covered the mouth of the vial. The remainder of the glove he twisted firmly around the cylinder to make a tight seal. He had practiced this motion an endless number of times before deciding on the method. To his relief, the vial wrapped perfectly. With the vial secure in his pocket, he shut the gate and replaced the padlock.

He stared at the luminous hands of his watch to confirm how his schedule was going. He would have sworn that five minutes had passed during that sequence of movements. One and a half minutes; he felt the weakness of relief.

As Walter left the hangar he hoped desperately that his stiff legs were producing something that resembled a casual walk. Only one step remained, but the metronome had quickened, thumping against the inner wall of his chest, tightening his belly muscles to force a recurrent threat of nausea at the back of his throat.

He was scared. God in heaven, he was scared. His terror affected a casual nonchalance as he paused at the door of the hangar housing Dobbs's P-39. He forced himself to stand there a minute, staring idly, before shoving the door those few inches that allowed him to slip inside.

Poised in the center of that neatly organized hangar the P-39 looked innocent enough, hardly like the death trap that Walter knew it to be.

Forcing his mind from other years, other P-39s, he clambered onto the wing and pulled open the tiny door to the plane. He didn't have to struggle into that narrow cockpit that he remembered as fitting like a badly cut glove. Leaning over, he pulled the head gear of Dobbs's oxygen system out into the light.

The face mask was heavy from the special microphone that Dobbs had installed. Walter's hands were uncertain. He cursed softly as he tried the second time to slip off the mask. The work went easily once the mask was free. Balancing himself against the plane, he forced the second surgical glove onto his right hand. With his gloved hand he unwrapped the vial and poured the parathion down the oxygen tube.

It was over. His hands trembled wildly as he fitted the oxygen tube back on the mask and restored the mask to where he had found it. Before he leaped down from the wing, he folded both contaminated gloves, along with the vial, inside the plastic envelope and put it into his pocket.

The disposal dump was between him and the trailer. One and a half minutes. He was almost home free. He had only the key to the storage room to replace, an easy enough task. He could just toss it on the desk beneath the keyboard as if it had fallen from its place. There might be a scramble when it was first looked for, but as careless as Mac was, that was even doubtful. Mac himself would probably slip the key back onto the hook without a second thought.

As Walter reached the disposal dump he pulled the plastic bag from his pocket without looking down. As he passed, he tossed it into the debris in the can. He stopped dead in his tracks. An unexplainable click of metal against metal had sounded from the can. Glancing down, he saw the yellow tag of the key disappearing along with the plastic bag into the mass of discarded clothing and contaminated containers. He caught his breath, feeling a surge of sweat spring to his face.

What a jackass trick. But done was done. Mac would just find that his key wouldn't work. Thank God it was Friday. The refuse would be removed early the next morning before there would be any reason to search the premises for a lost key.

The tremor that had started in his hands was all over his

body now. He walked a few feet and paused, struggling for control. One of the Stearmans was coming in. Grateful for an excuse, Walter shielded his eyes to watch the graceful deep angle of the plane's approach. He had forgotten how painful the extreme of fear could be, the softness in his joints, the involuntary rebellion of his body against his mind's discipline.

But now it was over.

Why in hell did he put himself through such drills as this? For a long time he had told himself it was a revenge he was taking for his mother's death. That was bullwash, idealistic bullwash. He did it for the high, shrill scream of danger that was only now winding down in his head. He tried to remember his mother's face and instead the sun had faded even the memory of her into a cloud of sparkling, spermlike motes of brilliance.

The only face he could see was the skull emblazoned on crossbones on the side of the storage pen, the same image that flashed in his mind when he had watched the films his army had seized from the Nazis. The final irony of all this brought an almost uncontrollable laugh to his lips.

He had chosen parathion for strictly empirical reasons. It was murderously toxic. It was toxic either in vapor or on contact. Once exposed to air, it would disperse, leaving no trace for the cause of the pilot error that would crash that P-39 as soon as Dobbs began to use his oxygen.

But the irony of his choice was absolute. "Shrader," he whispered to himself. It was the German chemist Shrader who started all this with his study of organic phosphorous compounds when Hitler was still a corporal. That was where parathion had come from. The Nazis knew what they had, a nerve gas they could use in their mission to conquer the world. But first it had to be tested. What more natural to a German than to use the inmates of the concentration camps as guinea pigs for these tests?

There was no way that Stanley Dobbs would escape. By ten

thousand feet he would have that mask on and flip on the oxygen flow. All the highly touted symptoms of the gas would be irrelevant. Schizophrenia, depression, all those failings of the human mind didn't matter. Dobbs would simply black out. A man who blacks out at ten thousand feet in a P-39 is a dead man.

Walter froze as Mac hailed him. Mac was hustling along with the empty mug in his hand, his shoulders rising and falling from the limp in his game leg.

"Thought you'd be back in the trailer by now," Mac said, catching up.

Walter grinned. "I had to look in on that fancy little Mick of ours. It's been too long since I had her out for a spin."

"Things are bound to settle down," Mac assured him. "It's like money in the bank knowing she's in there."

As they reached the corner of the trailer, Dobbs drove in.

"Now the party really begins," Mac said acidly.

"Hang in there, Mac," Walter said, his hand on Mac's shoulder.

But he found himself looking at Dobbs curiously as he got out of his car and stretched. It was as if he was already dead. It was funny to watch a dead man wipe his sunglasses and turn to wave at you.

17

Friday, May 3

Mac had been relieved to see Heinemann and Christa arrive early. A cumulative anger had been growing in him as the time neared for Dobbs's arrival. He knew damned well that Dobbs was only coming out to start another fight.

A pervasive weariness had settled on him since Rick's death, a sense of defeat that was unusual. Even his body was coming to pieces. He hadn't slept a whole night since Rick went down but had wakened, sweating from nightmares. Toby . . . his face changing into the face of the dead Sutter boy. Meg calling from the stoop at twilight and planes going down, one after another against the sing of wires. Of course it was the Camels, but he found it hard to draw a deep breath in the humid air and a new dull pain had started in the old wound in his leg.

He was old before his time. Old and alone. He had wakened that morning with Meg on his mind. Without getting out of his bunk he had reached for the phone and dialed her number.

Even as she answered he could hear a baby crying off there.

"What's the matter with that kid?" he asked.

"You woke him up calling," she said tersely. "Hang on a minute or I won't hear a word."

He recognized the singsong of her voice talking to the child as she carried him to the phone. He could see it, for God's sake, the way she had of folding a blanket around a baby so a peak came up at the back and dropped a point on top of the head. The kid was still snuffling, but the squalling had stopped. From her own voice he could see her swaying back and forth like she was rocking him standing up.

"So why was he still asleep?"

Her voice was exasperated. "He's been up once and had his bath. That was his morning nap." Then, gentler, "But you aren't spending all this money to know about his schedule."

Why had he called? "I hadn't heard what you decided."

"It didn't occur to me that you cared," she said.

He was about to explode that he didn't care, that he was only curious, but he remembered the dull click that had ended their last conversation.

"So anyway you got the kid," he said.

"Nobody fought me or I wouldn't have," she said. "My age and all."

"What's the matter with your age?"

There was silence for a moment. He could almost hear her thinking, then her voice softer and confused. The kid was sucking on something, probably his fist. He heard the faint grunting and the moist sounds behind her voice.

"Are you okay, Mac?" she asked. "You're not sick or anything, hurt?"

The concern got to him. In the old days he never left without her saying, "Be careful now," in that tone of voice.

He had fought it then, calling back, "Sure, Meg, I was going to go out and take a hundred chances." Now the concern was at the same time comforting and irritating, but he didn't want her to hang up, he wanted her to keep talking.

"I'm okay. It's awful busy here. Lots of stuff going on."

Suddenly stiff and formal. "I appreciate your taking the time to call."

"Wait," he said, trying to stall off her ending the conversation. "What do you call that kid?"

She laughed a little as if she was embarrassed. "Mostly Lover," she admitted.

"He must have a name on his birth certificate," he insisted.

"He does," she said quietly. "I just can't handle that."

"Not even telling me?" he asked after a minute.

"You probably guessed it," she said, her voice near tears.

"Is he really jug-eared?" he asked.

"The worst you ever saw," she said. "Mac, I'm worried about your bill."

He had gotten off then and laid there a long time putting in words that had been left out. The name had to be Toby, nothing else would bother Meg that much. She must be tight for money, too, to be worrying about his bill the whole time he talked. He wouldn't have to build much of a house there on that lot in Blakeslea. She and the kid could have a good safe life. Maybe she'd garden again like the old days, tomatoes and stuff to pad out the groceries.

He had decided to tell Heinemann about it, about the baby Toby had left and Meg and all, but there wasn't a chance. He had no more than finished up with Evert and was starting back to the trailer than he saw Dobbs pulling into the lot.

Mac expected to see the Texan in the car with Dobbs. Instead Dobbs was alone, getting out and stretching a minute as he glanced toward the trailer where Walter stood with Christa. God, that girl was tall and as slender as a wand, like Meg had been in the old days. Something must have been exchanged between them because the girl stepped back, disappearing into the trailer as if she had been sent.

"I thought there was someone you wanted us to meet," Mac told Dobbs right off.

"He'll be along in a while," Dobbs said. "I thought maybe the three of us needed some time to talk first."

Dobbs started walking toward the storage area where they had unloaded the Stearman that Rick died in. Mac went along willingly. If there were going to be harsh words, they needn't be broadcast to the ground crew or Cramar.

"Well, there she is," Heinemann said, stopping at the carcass of the plane.

"What's left of her," Dobbs said. "The FAA sure let you off easy with that one, Mac."

"What do you mean 'let me off, *me*'? I didn't hit that damned standpipe. Rick's not the first flyer in the world to hit a fixed obstacle either."

"I guess I was thinking of the safety record," Dobbs replied. "Two planes in a week?"

"This isn't getting us anywhere," Heinemann put in.

"That's what I'm saying," Dobbs went on. "Mac's the manager out here. Did you check this guy out or just take him on his papers? And that job where he died, did you ever fly that field and see how the ground obstacles are from the air?"

"Cool it, Dobbs," Heinemann said. "We're not out here for recriminations. You wanted to talk to us, you wanted us to see this new pilot fly. Let's get to it."

"There's more than that on my mind," Dobbs said. "We need to replace Rick, but we also need to turn this business around."

"We came to see your pilot fly but not to hire him, Dobbs. Mac and I have run the numbers every way. The cheap way is to hire a pilot with his own crate until we finish out the rice."

"I know what you said," Dobbs replied. "But I've figured out another alternative."

"Like what?" Heinemann asked with a warning glance at Mac.

"I would be willing to lease an agricultural plane myself and lend it to the company to be flown by our pilot. We could stay on schedule with a minimum expense to the firm."

"You what?" Heinemann said, his face tightening with disbelief. Mac was astounded to see a visible change in Heinemann's face. He looked harder all of a sudden, and his faint accent got stronger. His tone was sharply challenging. "Okay, Dobbs," he said. "Level with us. What's in this for you?"

Mac could see Dobbs was a little startled by Walter's response.

He smiled almost nervously and his tone turned light.

"Good God, Walter, don't blow off at me. It's my business as well as yours, you know. I was just looking ahead. There's the rice to wind up and then peaches right on its heels. You haven't figured on how much money we'd be losing."

"It ain't money we lose," Mac corrected him. "It's business. We make money flying, but we don't lose money when we don't fly. Even with Rick out we'll clear costs and make a decent profit. It's just that we handle more business with that slot filled."

Dobbs turned on him impatiently. "Don't tell me about money and business. You're a pilot, not a financier."

"Listen, Dobbs," Heinemann put in. "I don't get this at all. Why lease a plane and put a man on the payroll when that Stearman won't be ready to fly for almost a year? There must be a reason for you to give a profit gift like this to the firm."

Dobbs's friend couldn't have picked a worse time to come around the end of the hangar, but there he was, a tall, skinny guy with a Stetson pushed back from his leathery face. It had to be the same guy that Mary and the waitresses had described.

"I hope I'm not early," he said, his eyes on Dobbs. The slur of his accent knifed Mac's consciousness. Texas. That was Texas all right, the voices of the men who had flown with Toby and then buried him. Mac's mouth turned so dry that he couldn't have spoken if he wanted to.

When Dobbs introduced Jackson around he offered his hand to Heinemann but not to Mac. "Nice shop you got here," he told Mac, half grinning.

"I hadn't gotten around to telling my partners about you, Jackson," Dobbs said. He flipped open his flight bag and pulled out a sheaf of papers clipped together. "These will give you some idea of Jackson's qualifications."

"The problem," Heinemann began without looking at the papers, "the problem is that we don't need a pilot right now. This is no reflection on your qualifications, but you can see what decision needs to be made first."

Jackson nodded, his eyes on Dobbs, as Heinemann went on smoothly.

"Why don't you go back to the pilot's lounge in the nearest trailer there and have some coffee. Just tell Mrs. Cramar that I sent you."

Jackson barely hesitated before moving away. He walked with the gait of a cowboy, his shoulders a little hunched and his walk rolling.

"Now look here, Heinemann," Dobbs said. "That was pretty highhanded, I'd say. I scrape up a good, competent pilot and make commitments to him. I offer to provide a plane at no expense and you slam the door in both our faces."

"Nobody is slamming any doors." Heinemann raised his voice above the sound of the plane taxiing down the runway. "Let's do it the simple way, Dobbs. Let's bring in a pilot and a plane until Evert gets the Stearman up. Then we can talk about hiring a man."

Heinemann had begun to walk as he spoke, edging the group in the direction of the office. After a few steps, Dobbs stopped short like a man digging his heels in for a fight.

"No, by God. I have put up with all the mollycoddling of Mac that I intend to. This is a partnership, not some little Nazi dictatorship that you've set up. I say we need a pilot and that we need that pilot. Those men out there aren't made of steel. Men get sick. Men wear out. We need a relief pilot even if we don't have an extra plane."

"There's Mac here," Heinemann said. "When a crisis like that comes up, Mac can always take over."

"Mac," Dobbs scoffed. "Jackson can fly a ring about Mac when he flew his best."

Mac felt the blood tighten against his temples. "What in hell do you mean by that?"

"Come clean with us, Mac," Dobbs said. "When were you last in the air? Why, you haven't been able to fly a kite since that kid of yours burned the wires. You're through, Mac. We need a man who can fly and run this shop. You've had it."

Mac froze for a split second. It was like being stripped buff-naked with Heinemann looking on. He felt rather than heard the curse boil out of his throat as he leaped at Dobbs. The smash of Dobbs's jaw under his fist was satisfying. Then Heinemann had him by the back, pinning his arms in a solid grip.

Mac felt his strength draining from him as he stared back at Dobbs, whose eyes were as cold as steel.

"All right, Mac," Dobbs said softly. "Let's see you fly. Let's see you take a plane up and do half the things that a wet-eared kid out of flight school can do with his eyes shut. You're through, Mac. Try to be man enough to face it."

Through. Mac thought of his palms, the flesh there as soft as a woman's where the calluses had peeled off. All the nights came back in a rush, nights of wakening from sweat-drenched dreams of flying, the wind whistling past his face, tearing a long, hollow scream out of his throat.

He didn't trust himself to speak. Pulling himself from Heinemann's grip, he limped purposefully toward the hangar where the Mick was housed. He slid the door open with a resounding crash. The crewmen on a nearby truck stared in astonishment. Mac's own flight bag was on a shelf by the door. The crew was instructed to keep the plane gassed and in flying condition. By God, they better have done it because he had to go, right on the minute before the cold sweat spurting from his pores drenched his jumpsuit for that damned Dobbs to see.

"Give me a hand with this baby," he said to Heinemann as he kicked the block from under the plane. "I'm going to give this bastard a flying lesson."

"Come on, Mac," Heinemann said gently. "Settle down, both of you. We'll talk . . ."

Dobbs leaned against the open door of the hangar, waiting.

"Let him go, Heinemann," he urged. "We don't use that plane for anything but play anyway. If he smashes it, there will be no great loss to this company."

Heinemann whirled on Dobbs. Mac had never thought he'd see that cool man lose his self-control, but now it was close.

"Dobbs." Heinemann's voice was warning. "Lay off. You're making a fool of yourself. This whole thing is a fiasco. Let's sit down like sensible men and talk."

"Talk," Dobbs replied with a scoff. "You're no better than he is, Heinemann. You'd prattle on forever and let the business go down the drain. I can see why you don't want him to fly. You know as well as I do that he can't handle it. He's too old and scared to pull a stick."

Heinemann stared wordlessly at Dobbs, fury white around his mouth. Then he walked briskly to stand behind the other wing of the Stearman. Mac reached up to the wall rack for his parachute and Dobbs laughed.

"Look at you. You already know that if you come down it won't be on wheels."

Mac stared at him and turned back to the plane, leaving the chute on the wall.

"Come on, Mac," Heinemann urged. "Wearing a chute is no sign of cowardice; it's just good sense."

When Mac shook his head, Heinemann leaned his weight against the wing of the plane. The Stearman rolled out easily and Mac and Heinemann lined her up with the runway.

Mac was no sooner up than Heinemann climbed toward the passenger seat.

"What are you doing?" Mac shouted.

"You're taking me for a ride," Heinemann called back to him. "And believe me, this is the last shit we take off of that guy. Believe me."

Mac waited until Dobbs was safely out of range before he hit the starter on the Stearman. "Don't let that son of a bitch kill you," he heard Dobbs shout to Heinemann. The sweat was all the way through the jumpsuit so that it tugged at his shoulders and clung miserably to his crotch. The engine started, stalled, then started again, a roar rising from the belly of the plane that even drowned out Mac's heartbeat.

The last thing Mac saw as he teased the plane down the runway was Dobbs leaning against the hangar, looking like a man who had just won a jackpot.

18

May 3

Just the feel of the bucket seat of the Stearman under Mac's tail was enough to bathe him in a fresh sheet of clammy sweat. He locked his jaw hard as he rocked the plane along the runway. For the first time he didn't resent the prune trees he had torn out to lengthen the strip for Dobbs's P-39. It felt good to have plenty of room, to feel that strip solid under him as the plane gained momentum, its wings seeming to flutter with eagerness to take off.

He was scared. By God, he was scared, but that wasn't the same thing as yellow. Any man worth his salt was scared once in a while, but yellow was a stain on the soul. There had been plenty of times during the war, and quite a few since, that terror had wiped his mouth dry of spit and melted his knee joints; but no man could accuse Mac Maguire of being yellow.

He looked at the back of Heinemann's head, wishing to God that Heinemann had taken a helmet. It had been one cool gesture, the way Heinemann had climbed in without a parachute, but there was no call for him to have his head blown off going without a helmet.

The Stearman lifted easily into the wind. The sky, usually a clear, unspotted blue out here in the valley, was showing some signs of trouble, a cloud bank off to the northwest. But it was still May and a rain could come. The last number Mac had heard on wind velocity was five, an easy number to handle in this plane at any altitude.

All four hundred and fifty horses roared on the climb. At three thousand feet Mac leveled off. He made two gentle clearing turns, one right and one left, just to make damned sure that the sky was clean. Then he dropped the nose and listened as the wind built up to a shriek in the wing wires, then smoothly pulled up and rocked the wings over, applying the opposite rudder to keep the plane from yawing and to hold its nose up. As the plane rolled past forty-five degrees he eased off the back pressure. When the horizon swung vertical again, he reversed and rolled the plane over on its other side.

Dropping the nose, he dived to build up momentum for one perfect, gentle, lazy Eight.

Christ.

"Okay," he thought, the hard ball of terror beginning to soften in his belly. "I know you, girl," he murmured to the roar of the engine. "I know all about you."

It was true. He was suddenly as sensitive to the plane as if she were a woman. He knew her flexibilities and her strengths, those unexpected weaknesses that could drag a man down with her if he forgot, even for a moment, at the wrong time.

The feel of the responsive machine under his hand and the sweetness of the slicing blue air past his face startled him into involuntary laughter. God, what a clown he had been. How many months had he waited on the ground? How had he let the false panic of nightmares rob him of his own world? You were born to fly, you crazy bastard, he told himself in exultation. Never mind your nightmare, never mind Toby's wires; flying was one man, one hour, one patch of sky.

As he saw Heinemann's hand raised in an easy salute, Mac grinned to himself. So Mac couldn't fly, was that what Dobbs thought? Dobbs was going to get a goddamned air show. Then let him cram that lanky Texan down anybody's throat.

Mac dived until he could feel the roar all the way through his bones before he flipped the plane into wide, graceful aileron rolls, one right, one left, and then nosed down to enter a perfect Immelmann, and headed back over the field.

It was strange how unimportant Dobbs seemed when he was up here with the Stearman responding to his body like it was sewed on. Mac dropped the nose and entered the dive for a sweeping Cuban Eight. As he pulled up, the positive G's rammed him back into his seat, giving him that locked-in sensation of winged power that nothing, by God, nothing else in the world could touch.

Mac whistled softly through his teeth. He could feel the great looped circles he had flown like ribbons of movement against the sky. Even Heinemann felt good. Mac saw his right hand rise, fingers forming a circle of congratulations against the blue.

He could see the knot of people gathered on the ground by the trailer. He couldn't pick out the figures, but the group had to include that goddamned cowboy as well as Cramar and Christa. He wagged a wing in salute and saw Heinemann waving too. A working sprayer pulled in beneath him, landing on the runway and taxiing toward the loading area.

Mac realized that his eyes were streaming in spite of the goggles. He knew he could fly this crate all day and all night. What a fool he had been to psych himself out like that. Being a one-handed operator, his right hand was beginning to sting from his pressure on the stick. Enough was enough until he got those good old horny calluses built back up. Just this one more maneuver and he would be ready to stand eye to eye with Dobbs and tell him to go to hell.

Mac leaned hard against his seatbelt to shout to Heinemann above the wind. "Hang on there," he yelled exultantly. He saw Heinemann's nod, an easy movement that implied that he was ready for anything Mac wanted to throw him.

Mac dived at red line to pick up enough air speed for an outside loop. That would give them both those beautiful negative G's that would ram their bellies in under their chins like a roller coaster ride. He rolled inverted, shoved the stick forward for the outside loop and shot into the curving climb.

Stanley Dobbs realized that the sky, which had been clear early in the afternoon, was developing threatening clouds. Damned nuisance. If the forecasted rain blew in on that rising wind, his air show on Sunday could be postponed. It was too early to worry about that. He shaded his eyes against the sun and waited by the trailer watching the old Irishman show off. Even Evert had come from the shop to stand beside them.

"That Mac up there?" he asked in disbelief.

At Cramar's nod he snorted and then spat, his mouth curled in a grin. "That old bastard will never grow up." Then he remembered, and glancing around guiltily, mumbled, "Excuse, ma'am" to no one in particular. He walked away looking a little hangdog but keeping his eye on the plane above.

Dobbs inwardly cursed as he watched the plane. He couldn't believe that such a good idea could have failed so utterly. The idea had come like a bolt from the blue. His careful plan to fulfill his mission by executing Walter Heinemann during the night before the air show went down the drain with this "trip" Walter was leaving on so unexpectedly. He was still fighting his frustration when he had arrived at the field to have Heinemann and Mac so clearly aligned against him.

It was when he was letting Heinemann know that Mac was no longer flying that he remembered. The last time Dobbs himself had taken up that Stearman he had checked the seat belts to see that they were secure. The catch on the passenger seat had acted strangely. It held at first only to give way after a sudden pressure. It was a gamble that Heinemann would go up with Mac. If he went, Dobbs was sure that Mac would give Heinemann enough negative G's to throw him out. He had even goaded them about chutes and was lucky that Heinemann was too mad to be thinking straight. And now even that scheme had misfired.

"It's still all right," he assured himself. His original plan could be worked any time after Heinemann's return. With things the way they were, he always had an excuse to come out to the valley. His gun was ready. He had an extra can of gas so he wouldn't have to stop in the middle of the night. Every exigency was covered. One weekend was as good as the next. But it would have been a real coup if he could have successfully jumped his own gun with that flawed seatbelt.

Now if Mac would just quit showing off and bring the plane down. He watched Mac waggle the field like a kid. Jesus, what a ham. Dobbs had turned back to the trailer to refill his mug of coffee when he realized that Mac was taking the Stearman into yet another dive.

"What does that crate do?" Jackson asked, sounding a little impressed.

"A hundred and seventy," Dobbs told him tersely.

The plane was only a few hundred yards past the strip, still over the prune orchard. Right then, when the plane was at red line, Mac rolled over and pushed into an inverted loop. As Mac brought the plane's nose up, Dobbs felt himself flinch. It was strange the way that flinch went through his body even before his mind identified the object that hurtled from the plane to plunge downward within the first twenty degrees of the outside loop.

The chilling silence ended as abruptly as it began. A high shrill scream sounded close to Dobbs's ear. It didn't sound like a human scream at all, more like primitive pain being transformed into sound. Dobbs turned, blinking his sun-glazed eyes.

The scream was coming from Cramar, whose mouth had become an open wound in her face. Her eyes were buried by balled fists as if she meant to rub from her brain the sight that was burned on it. But the screaming didn't stop, only rose and fell with gasps of pained breath.

Heinemann's girl, her face ashen, caught Cramar by the shoulders and guided her toward the trailer. Evert had already thrown a boy off a truck in the lot and was kicking the motor to life.

As he ran to catch onto the truck with Evert, Dobbs shouted back to Jackson. "Call somebody, the police, an ambulance . . . somebody."

Even as he ran he could see Mac circling the spot where the faulty seatbelt had failed Heinemann. Mac had pulled out of the loop as fast as he dared and now he was circling the spot, down and down in a narrowing spiral.

Jesus, Dobbs thought. He can't be ten feet above those trees. He clung to the truck barreling along between the rows of prune trees. Mac continued to circle in graceful despairing circles above the spot where Heinemann's body had disappeared into the trees.

19

Blakeslea, California, Saturday, May 11

The county courthouse in Blakeslea was built when light oak was in vogue. The furnishings of the courtroom had originally had a faintly yellowish tone that colored the light from the narrow windows flanking the judge's bench. It was written in the local paper at the time that this phenomenon "bathed the process of justice in the golden light of truth."

Time and negligence had dulled this color to a deep muddy brown except where the citizens of Blakeslea had inadvertently kept the county property polished with their trousers and sleeves.

Stan Dobbs slipped into his place on the bench with relief. It seemed to him that Sheriff Prentice had taken his own sweet time getting this inquest set up. But nothing about Walter Heinemann's death had been handled with the brisk efficiency he had learned to expect in his own part of California. The sheriff's men had come at once with the FAA investigators hard on their heels, but they were still working over the death scene until very late that night. The threatened storm moved in about seven. By eight o'clock the slow, drumming rain was pounding on the roof of the office trailer that the sheriff used as a temporary headquarters.

Dobbs had called Ginger the first chance he had to tell her what was going on. As it turned out, the TV had already been airing the story, complete with shots of the prune orchards and Mac Maguire's shocked and anguished face. At that time she had also heard that, due to the severity of the weather front, the Sunday air show had been postponed for a week.

"Then you'll be home soon?" she asked.

"Whenever this is settled down here," he told her. "Don't wait up."

When he was finally released by the sheriff it was with the caution that he would be recalled to testify as a witness at the coroner's inquest.

"When will that be?" Dobbs had asked.

"Later in the week sometime," Sheriff Prentice guessed. "The labs don't work on Sunday and we have to get the material in there and have it processed. There'll be some questioning around."

"What in hell is that for?" Dobbs had challenged. "There were all of us watching at the strip as well as the rancher who saw the accident from the road. That makes ten witnesses to what happened." That of course didn't count the sheriff himself and the crowd of curious who crowded into the prune orchard before Heinemann's body was cold.

"That's my responsibility as coroner," Prentice told him. "And as sheriff too, I might add."

"Then I'll wait to hear from you," Dobbs replied, retreating.

Not even the long dark drive home in the pouring rain had been able to depress him. Walter Heinemann was dead. His mission had been a swift and dramatic success. The only thing the inquest could prove was that a human body given four times its weight in negative G's would strike the ground from three thousand feet with sufficient force to pulverize every bone in that body.

But he still wanted the inquest over and the books closed. He couldn't settle his mind to anything with the inquest still hanging.

He had come early. Aside from a few ranchers smoking outside the door, there was little suggestion of anything afoot. He watched a bird-legged woman enter the room from a door at the left of the judge's bench. Her air of self-importance didn't allow her to acknowledge his presence. After shuffling the papers on the table, she frowned, altered the position of a lamp and nodded stiffly to a court reporter as she left.

A heavy-bodied fly droned against the high window behind the judge's bench. Dobbs watched its pounding search up and down the glass, hypnotized by the insect's blind persistence. He noticed with a start that the room behind him was filling with people and the jury filing into the box.

Dobbs studied the faces of the jury panel. These were citizens who, as Sheriff Prentice explained, "had expressed a willingness to be of service to the county." They were a mixed bag at best, mostly of retirement age except for one pale young man whose posture suggested a severe health problem.

A visible ripple of interest alerted Dobbs to the arrival of Christa Cove. She stood alone in the doorway, tall and remarkably slender against the light from the hall. She was wearing either a dress that looked like a coat or the other way around, he couldn't tell. But it was of the soft muted green that set off her strange-colored eyes. She was a showstopper, Dobbs thought uneasily. Damn Heinemann. Dobbs was astonished to see Christa's eyes seek his face. Without a change of expression, she walked down the aisle to slide into the seat beside him.

He had no more than murmured a greeting to her than Sheriff Prentice rose, looking amplified in his triple role as sheriff, coroner and judge.

Covertly Dobbs studied Mac seated among the others from the Flying Mick: Evert, his shoulders straining at the seams of a gray jacket, Manuel and Orville and the boy Jamie whose last name Dobbs could never remember. Mac's freshly shaven cheeks and chin were lighter than the rest of his sun-darkened face. Mostly he stared at his hands clenching and unclenching in his lap. He was a beaten man. It showed in the angle of that bull neck. Handling him should present no problems from here on out, but there was still the inquest to go through.

The purpose of the coroner's inquest as stated by Sheriff Prentice was to examine the cause of Walter Heinemann's death. The unusual nature of the accident coupled with certain discrepancies in the accounts of witnesses had prompted the coroner to examine the evidence by inquest.

This mildly suggested reference to foul play stirred Mac from his apathy to glance thoughtfully at the sheriff.

The report of the coroner's investigation seemed unnecessarily tedious. Dobbs decided that Prentice was bucking for political advancement and this was the best airing he might get. After all, the accident had been given the same gruesome excess of coverage as all violent deaths are entitled to. The coroner's assistant was also a dog whose day had come and he missed none of its advantages.

The exhibits included a carefully drawn diagram of the angle of Heinemann's descent from the plane followed by a series of pictures in which Heinemann stared back in death from the undergrowth of the prune orchard. Briefly stated, the pathological and microscopic findings betrayed no evidence of drugs or alcohol in the cadaver, no discernible signs of wound such as would have been inflicted by knife or gun, and that all available evidence indicated that Walter Heinemann was living and of sound body when he was ejected from the seat of the Stearman. A wire cutter found in the dead man's jacket pocket had inflicted the only wound on the body not explainable by his fall onto the rough terrain of the orchard.

In tedious sequence the witnesses to the accident were called.

Mac seemed unable to rouse himself from a weak-voiced lethargy that laid his arms limply along the arms of the witness chair. As the questions continued, he rallied, finally answering in the more bluff, forceful manner characteristic of him.

"Hell, yes, there was a fight," he replied to the sheriff's question. "Dobbs had come out there trying to run the shop no matter what Heinemann and I thought. He was spoiling for a fight and I pasted him."

A murmur of supportive response stirred through the courtroom, but Mac ignored it. Dobbs had to give Mac credit. Mac described the argument fairly. The words he quoted sounded like his own even though Dobbs himself would have been unable to recall that clearly what he had shouted in the heat of his anger.

"So the entire flight took place in response to a sort of dare?" the sheriff pressed.

Dobbs felt his own shallow intake of breath. That hick sheriff was stumbling a little close to the truth there. But Mac himself eased Dobbs off the hook. He squared his jaw, glared across the room at Dobbs and spoke scathingly.

"Hell, no. He said I couldn't fly and I, by God, showed him that I could."

"So you and Heinemann readied for the flight. Were you wearing a parachute?"

"No," Mac grumbled.

"Is it your habit to do that sort of flying without a chute?"

"Hell, no," Mac's words poured out, seeming driven by an urgent need to explain. "Heinemann and I both always wear chutes, but we were both mad as hell. During the busy season when that plane isn't used much, the chutes are taken out and hung on the hangar wall. It's better for them than lying in the seats with the air moist and hot."

"Then they were available," the sheriff said. "All you had to do was pull them off the wall and put them on."

Mac nodded. "That's right. But with Dobbs goading us the

way he was, we couldn't have used the chutes without it looking like we thought he was right about our being in danger with me at the stick."

"Then your failure to wear chutes was a sort of gesture to show your assurance," the sheriff suggested.

Mac nodded, looked confused, and then shook his head. "Good God, Prentice. Neither of us had any idea that there was anything wrong with that plane. Heinemann himself got it fixed up for just the kind of flying I was doing. He didn't hold any horses on that either. That baby is even equipped with an inverted fuel system to feed gas when you're flying upside down."

The sheriff paused. He read his next question from a slip in front of him. Someone who knew flying must have helped him with that one, Dobbs decided, maybe even someone from the FAA. The jurors were completely lost, listening with the guilty attention of the utterly confused.

Mac shook his head emphatically. "If somebody tried to jimmy that belt on purpose, they would never have brought it off. Nobody's clever enough to fix a belt to hold a hundred-and-eighty-pound man through some maneuvers and pitch him on a different one."

Prentice did not explain what expert examined the seat belt clasp after Mac's choppy landing, but the photograph showed a malfunction in the pin of the central catch where the shoulder harness connected with the seat belt itself.

After studying the pictures and handing them back, Evert supported Mac's statement. "It's right there in the picture for anyone to see. That catch can slip. It takes a pretty heavy jolt, but it's flawed enough to slip when the jerk comes right."

"Could this flaw have been arranged deliberately?"

"Oh, hell, no," Evert said with astonishment. "You'd get into a pretty piece of physics trying to do that. The thing just decided to go and went, like all man-made things do sooner or later."

But Dobbs had to give the sheriff his due. It was as if he sensed something and was unsure what trail to follow. He went back to Rick's fatal flight, recalling a comment of Dobbs's that he had overheard or had quoted to him.

"Was there a question in your mind about the way Maguire was having the planes maintained?"

Dobbs hedged, not so much wary of his oath as concerned that he was too close to being home free to muddy the water.

"It seemed to me that we had too many problems," Dobbs said mildly. "I probably mentioned that along with other possible factors. Like pilot fatigue."

It was to Jamie, the boy of all work, sometimes swamper, sometimes flagger, that Prentice put the final crucial question from Dobbs's point of view.

"Presuming that it had been possible to tinker with that seat belt in the way that has been described, do you know any reason why anyone would wish violence to Walter Heinemann?"

The boy's eyes widened in amazement. "You mean somebody out there wanting to off him?"

The sheriff nodded, his amusement visible in his eyes.

"No way." The boy shook his head. "If there was that kind of bad blood it was only between the boss, Mac, and that Dobbs over there."

When Dobbs returned to the court after recess, the crowd had thinned out. The fly had succumbed to whatever makes flies tumble dry and helpless on window sills with their legs clawing at the sky.

By midafternoon the last of the witnesses spoke to a nearly empty room. The sheriff, self-conscious with his gavel, dismissed them pending the verdict of the jury.

Christa had left the courtroom a few minutes before it was dismissed. Evert and the others had apparently returned to the Flying Mick. As Dobbs walked to his car there was only a knot of ranchers left of the courtroom crowd. These men were grouped around Mac, who was holding a court of his own on the steps of the building. As Dobbs passed within a few feet of them they lapsed into silence, following him with hostile eyes until he turned the corner.

All right, he fumed furiously. It was him and Mac now. The verdict could only go one way no matter what the sheriff suspected. Another closed book on a perfect crime. Now it was Mac's turn.

An orange Volkswagen was parked by Dobbs's car in the community parking lot. He was startled to recognize the woman standing beside it as Christa Cove. She was standing serenely, staring off across the street as if her mind was a million miles away.

Dobbs approached her almost hesitantly, but she turned at his coming and he found himself suddenly self-conscious with her strange eyes full of his own. God, that woman had a mouth . . . perhaps . . .

"I thought you had already left," he said, interrupting his own thoughts.

"I was waiting for you," she said quietly.

She smiled and a whole range of wonderful possibilities opened in Dobbs's mind. After all, she had been Heinemann's girl, and Heinemann was dead.

"That was thoughtful," he said, trying to figure out what could be coming next.

"That was a beautiful job," she said, still smiling. "I wanted you to know that I realized that it was a really beautiful job."

Dobbs frowned. "The testimony?" he asked, then shrugged. Why in hell was he so edgy with her? It was like a woman to make senseless conversation when she was trying to get a man's attention. "I only told it like it was."

"Not the testimony," she said quietly. "Walter Heinemann."

"Walter Heinemann," he parroted, both confused and edgier than before.

She nodded and caught at her lip with her teeth, ducking her head a little as if in reaffirmation of what she had said.

He tensed himself against a sense of sudden panic. The

woman was only being obscure. She can't possibly know what she is saying.

"Very ingenious," she went on calmly. "Quick and clean and very professional. No one else at all has figured out what happened."

The sudden chill along his spine was real now. His brain registered money. God in heaven. What had she seen? Did she have enough to make blackmail stick? His voice came out brusquer than he intended.

"I don't read you at all, Miss Cove," he said, forcing a new emotional distance with his tone.

Then she laughed. Her long, slim hand was on his arm. "Don't be like that, Stanley Drobot," she said languidly. "It's a compliment to you that I came to deliver in person."

He could feel the warmth of her hand through his jacket sleeve. That warmth seemed unreal against his own coldness.

"Maybe you would feel better if I quoted the exact words of the message I received from headquarters," she suggested lightly. She pursed her lips briefly as if to jog her memory and then spoke solemnly in a stilted, almost mocking tone. "Congratulate Agent Stanley Drobot, also known as Stanley Dobbs, on the swift and successful completion of his mission. A great danger has been removed from his own mission. Tell him also that his comrades are pleased."

Dobbs stared dumbly as she slid under the wheel of the VW and pulled the seat belt across her slim body. She had the door shut and the car into neutral as she smiled up at him.

"Pleased," she repeated, her voice barely audible above the racket of the car's engine.

He tried to cling to the window ledge of the car to say more to her, but she backed out too swiftly. She didn't wave or even glance back. She was gone, just like that. The last he saw of her was the almost imperious tilt of her head as she slowed for the turn at the corner.

Because there was nothing else to do, Dobbs unlocked his

car and got in. He felt strangely weak and his hands were trembling helplessly.

God in heaven. It all made incredible, powerful sense. They had sent her, of course. You didn't see women every day like that one. They'd sent her to check up on Heinemann and found out something dangerous about him. Then she had known about Dobbs himself all the time. While she stood there watching Heinemann's body plunge out of that plane she already knew. Cool.

When his muscles relaxed enough, he started the car and drove it out to that shoulder west of town and parked under the trees. He took a long drink out of the flask and just sat there, staring at the endless colors of the valley sunset.

In a way he had been robbed. He realized for the first time what an intense, gut-deep pleasure he would have gotten from the sight of Heinemann's face dissolving into shattering bone and blood right there in front of him. But it was over and they were pleased.

"Your comrades are well pleased," he whispered out loud to himself.

20

Saturday, May 17

Mac knew by six o'clock that Saturday morning that the day would be a heller. The sun rolled up, hot and determined, with the sky a bleached blue behind it. At least there wasn't any wind. Not that he wouldn't have liked a breath of cool air to draw, but the heat was enough for the pilots to fight without wind, too. Unheard of things went wrong right off the bat. His dealer sent out an order of pesticides on an early run. After Mac signed for it, he pulled the key down and went to unlock the enclosure so the dealer could legally unload it.

Damned if something hadn't gone wrong with the lock. For a few minutes he wondered if he had the wrong key, but it had to be the right one, marked with the yellow tab and all. Finally he took the whole damned lock off with a cutter from Evert's shop. Not being able to leave the place unsupervised, he had to wait out there until Jamie could ride into town for a new lock and key.

The rest of the day he spent at his desk layering the ceiling of the trailer with dense smoke that even reddened his own eyes. Invoices, orders and check sheets flowed past him in an untidy stream, getting processed by some disengaged part of himself that seemed unlinked with the despair of his conscious mind.

He told himself that his growing tiredness was due to the work.

He promised himself that after dinner and a good night's sleep he would shake off this exhaustion. He knew he was lying.

Part of the problem had to be frustration. Sheriff Prentice had promised to call when the coroner's jury reached a conclusion. The pressure of waiting had become a mountain that he carried by sheer force of will. The last order of the Sunday schedule had been clipped to the flight board when the call finally came. It was three minutes after four, he noticed, as he took the phone from Cramar.

"I thought you'd forgotten," he told Prentice. "What in hell took them so long?"

Prentice's explanation sounded a little lame.

"They had all that stuff to go through." Prentice's tone was uneasy. "The diagrams and the reports and all that technical stuff. You don't have to come," he reminded Mac. "It's only a formality, them bringing in their verdict."

"What if you need to arrest me?" Mac asked bluntly.

"Now come on, Mac," Prentice said. "I told the foreman to figure on four-thirty. That give you enough time?"

"Plenty," Mac told him. "I'll be there."

He avoided Cramar's eyes as he pulled his jacket off the coat rack by the keyboard. All week Cramar had worn a hangdog look. He was afraid to meet her eyes for fear she'd start that squalling she was doing when he brought down the Stearman without Walter Heinemann.

Prentice acted like he didn't know why Mac wanted to be there. The sheriff must understand that "wanting" had nothing to do with it. Mac needed to be there so he could turn the whole affair in his mind and say, "It's over, finished." There were enough unanswered questions and unexplained feelings without adding that one.

There was that son of a bitch Dobbs for instance.

He hadn't seen Dobbs since the inquest. Mac had been braced for Dobbs to come on strong like he always had. He had expected Dobbs to attack him from the witness box like he had from almost the first day around the shop. But no, Dobbs had let on as if it had been berries and cream with the three of them at the Flying Mick from the first.

The same Dobbs who had ragged him incessantly about aircraft maintenance had sworn on a Bible that the malfunction of that seat belt didn't reflect any negligence on Mac's part. He even played down the fight out by the hangar as "a few overheated words between partners and friends." Mac writhed, just thinking about it. Dobbs had been a damned alley cat throwing dirt like crazy to cover his own crap and everybody else's.

Mac should have called Dobbs's hand even if it meant dragging a lot of dirty linen into court. But he had been so stunned at the way Dobbs was acting that he didn't think of it. Some reason hung just beyond the corner of Mac's understanding and he couldn't think fast enough to catch it . . . then or now.

But sooner or later he had to sit down with Dobbs. He had tightened the schedules until there was no give left and they were still falling behind with Rick out of the line. A decision had to be made and Dobbs had to be in on it.

Sunday afternoon was the logical time. Dobbs was planning to fly out early to take part in the air show that had been cancelled by the storm that came with Heinemann's accident the week before. Dobbs would bring the plane back in late that afternoon. That would be the time to catch him and sit down with the bastard and iron things out.

Mac swerved the truck to avoid a Lab pup prancing along in

the dust of the road. A painful thud hit his belly as how close he had come to hitting the animal. God, would it ever end?

Toby. Then Rick. Now Heinemann. The edginess crawled along his spine. His mother, Katie Maguire, had called it his "Irish." There was no point in denying the shiver of apprehension that waked him at night and brought him up wide-eyed and sweating in the morning.

All that time his Irish had been trying to tell him and he hadn't listened. Now he was paying. But it wasn't over. There was still something wrong.

Back when he had dusted all the time like the others, he remembered making passes on a slope with everything going fine. Then a wind shear would hit that nearly tore the stick out of his hand. That was something a man could lock his hands onto and fight. This wasn't anything you could control with your good reflexes and the seat of your pants. It sort of hung there, waiting for you to look away so it could strike.

Like Heinemann. No warning at all. The seconds that preceded Heinemann's fall replayed themselves endlessly in his brain.

He had felt so high, so full of himself. He would perform that one last maneuver before he took Heinemann down. He remembered seeing the needle crawling to red line as he dived with the wind howling through the guy wires in the wings. Heinemann had raised his hand in that lazy, approving way.

The back of Heinemann's neck was there in front of him as he went into the roll and brought his nose up for the climb. Then it was like the shills at Reno said, "Now you see it . . . now you don't."

There should have been a thud, at least a vibration from the frame where that seat belt was bolted in. Nothing. There was only that stretch of air where Heinemann's head had been and a crunch of panic in his own belly. In the dream he'd always been screaming. If there was a scream it had burst from his throat without his knowing it.

There was nothing. Only the wind howling and that empty

seat as he pulled out of that outside loop and spiraled down to look for what was left of Heinemann after a three-thousand-foot drop.

Mac fished for his handkerchief to wipe off the sheen of cold sweat. What in hell was his mother's Irish good for if it couldn't warn a man for twenty seconds of pure hell?

Mac climbed the courthouse steps slowly, dragging his lame leg a little by the top. The foot traffic was all against him. The offices were closed and their clerical help was streaming out of the building. Most of the girls nodded as they passed. Some of the prettier ones even smiled.

Mac searched their faces for someone he knew, anyone. He liked thinking that Blakeslea was home to him. He liked thinking the townspeople knew him for what he was, rough maybe but not a guy to take chances with another man's life. But the word *negligence* hung there like a seven-foot question rolled out in white smoke. Was there something he could have done? He was alive and Heinemann was dead. Who was to blame?

The great thing would have been to be able to blame the whole event on Dobbs. It was Dobbs who had brought that Texan out, spoiling for a fight. It was Dobbs who had goaded them both to go up without chutes. He couldn't cop out like that. Why would Dobbs want Heinemann dead? Like Jamie had admitted under oath, the bad blood had been between Dobbs and himself.

Mac's footsteps echoed in the deserted hall. Even the courtroom was almost empty with only some regulars and a boy from the paper with a camera hanging around his neck.

Mac dropped onto a seat to wait while Prentice and the jury found their places. The foreman rose and exchanged a look of mutual relief with the man at his right.

"The decision of this jury," he began. Mac listened carefully. This was what he had come for. This was what he had held his breath for the whole week. He wanted to hear that the law had run its course, that it had found the death of Walter Heinemann an act of God that James Maguire had no part in. They couldn't say that too many times to please him.

Phrases flowed past Mac's head without penetrating his mind. "Freak accident," he heard. "Functional failure." And at the very end, "Insufficient evidence of criminal negligence to warrant further investigation."

When it was over, Prentice motioned Mac back to his office. Once there he poured Mac a shot of whiskey out of the paper-wrapped bottle from his bottom drawer. The whiskey burned all the way down without warming Mac. He realized he wasn't even surprised. He had felt this coming, this sense of being turned all the way to stone. Jesus, he could take anything but that, anger, pain, anything but this deadness of spirit. When Prentice filled the cup again, Mac swallowed it down numbly. Then he rose and shook Prentice's hand. "Thanks anyway," he told him.

"Twelve good men and true," Prentice said uneasily, his voice rising a little. "Not that it proves anything."

Mac just looked at him.

Prentice slid the bottle back into the drawer and flipped a key in the lock. "Life is a bitch," he said. "That's this lawman's considered opinion." Then he brightened. "Where are you going from here?"

Mac hesitated. "I thought I'd stop at Mary's for a bite." Dobbs would probably be at the strip sometime between now and dark looking over his plane. He'd stay away from there until he was sure Dobbs had gone to hole up in his motel room.

Prentice nodded. "That's good. Len Frank came by right after I called you. He'd missed you at the Flying Mick and had come here looking. He told me to tell you that he would hang around Mary's until you came by. He wants a word with you."

"I'll see him," Mac nodded.

The lights of the courthouse went off automatically at five sharp. The dimness turned the hall into a long, blunt tunnel whose end was cut off with that square flatness of solid wall.

"Hang in there," Prentice called after him.

Those had been Heinemann's words, too. Mac stood in the dark a long minute before starting his uneven progress toward the stairs.

21

Saturday, May 17

You could drive to Mary's Steakhouse blindfolded, Mac thought. In fact you could drive to it with nothing but your nose. Sure the music would help lead you with that crazy thrum from the machine that somebody always had quarters for. And you could watch the glow of red coming day and night out there in the parking lot. But the thing that led you to Mary's was the smell, the rich, burned smell of melted drops of beef fat and blood spitting on those white hot coals. And always the faintly sour smell of beer that had soaked into those wooden floors so long that if a man was to dig up underneath, he'd find the moles were hiccoughing.

Mac saw Len Frank's pickup in the lot and pulled his own in beside it. LUCKY FRANK RANCH was painted across the side, dark blue letters on a white background. Len's boy had painted that sign along with the one that was on the road to

Frank's spread. The boy had come back from Vietnam and gone down to Davis to go to veterinary college.

Mac had figured him to be a San Francisco adman some day, but the boy shook his head. "I need to make a 180-degree turn, Mac," he said. "All the way around. I'm going to save lives instead of destroying them."

"But why animals instead of people?" Mac had asked. The family had a dog and a mess of cats, but Frank was a rice-grower and never had a head of stock on his place that Mac knew of.

"I'll know that I'll heal something worth saving," the boy had replied. He had never talked that way before Vietnam.

There was a streaking of color against the sky already and the sun not all the way down. Mac opened the truck door and sat there looking at the sky through the newly leafed trees. It was peaceful out there. A flock of round-bodied birds toenailed the telephone wire, wobbling back and forth when one of them shifted along the line.

The sky's color reminded Mac of the pictures his mother used to take off calendars and hang in the bedroom hall. One of them had an angel all in white with its skirts folded close and the longest toes you ever saw. His mother, Katie Maguire, was mighty fond of that picture. She'd stop sweeping there to stand and stare at it.

But all the Maguire women believed in angels. Meg herself did and would argue at the top of her lungs if he kidded her about it.

But there was no teasing Katie Maguire about angels. In fact, after he was fifteen he avoided the subject when he could. That year Jim Norman rented his pasture to Skip Jensen, letting him tie down his plane between the little air shows he gave around that part of Pennsylvania and Ohio. The plane was a Standard, a spunky little biplane with an engine that sounded like it was making popcorn. But it got itself up and flew. It was easy for a kid who had been running a tractor since he was eight to learn to fly. What was hard was to get together the five bucks that Jensen charged for his lessons.

And getting around Katie Maguire.

"The only person outside of heaven who ever used wings was the devil himself," she told him. "And he was thrown out, remember. It's the devil's thing to do, getting up there with no single idea but to fall back down and kill yourself."

"What about angels?" he had asked.

She started for him with the broom. "The day you turn angel, I'll give you the five dollars meself," she told him.

And Katie Maguire never gave up her fight against his flying any more than Meg had. They were cut of a piece that way.

He stood in the fragrant air, staring at the phone booth outside the restaurant. Meg. Even if the jury had given him the cleanest bill of health in the world, there was still Dobbs to fight. Dobbs had money, prestige, and could buy lawyers all the way from here to the ocean if he needed them. Maybe it was time for him to get out, take his share and build a place on that lot he had bought for Toby. He rattled the coins in his pocket and came up with the right one.

Would you believe the kid was squalling?

"What nap did I wake him up from this time?" Mac asked.

She laughed softly. "He's in bed for the night. Or would be if he could blow his nose."

"Got a cold or is he just a naturally snotty-nosed kid?"

"Mac!" The tone was reproof, but there was laughter behind it. "It's one of those wet cold springs here," she explained.

"It's hot here and sunny," Mac told her.

Silences that long are expensive and her voice came a little breathless. "Mac, really now, are you all right?"

"I've been better," he admitted after a minute.

"Been down with something?" Her voice was solicitous. "Are you eating right?"

"Probably not," he conceded. "I lost one of my partners, a man I really liked."

Instant darkness in her tone. The Irish and death. "Oh, my dear," she breathed. Then hopefully, "An old man."

"Young," he told her. "An accident."

She would be thinking of it but wouldn't ask.

"I'll miss him," Mac said. "A man misses people from his life."

The baby had snuffled into a low rhythm of sobbing.

"This sun out here would dry up that kid's cold," he said. When she didn't answer, he went on. "Meg, I got a place here. It's not a place really, more just a lot a place would fit on. We could fence the yard and put in a garden."

Her tone was drier than the road at his back. "That's a lot of expense to cure a boy's sniffles."

He was sweating now. Any step he took now he was locked into.

"For God's sake quit that cat and mousing," he roared at her. "I'm asking you to come out and bring the kid. We can raise him here like no place else. But by God I'm not giving up flying."

Another one of those long silences. He could see Cramar checking the account of the Flying Mick where he had told the operator to charge it. Her eyebrows would rise and wriggle before she put that check by the amount.

"You didn't swear at me the first time you asked me to come be wife to you," she finally said.

"I didn't know you that well then."

"Only one thing. Is it really the boy you want or both of us?"

"My God, woman. No, wait, don't hang up, Meg."

"A woman misses people from her life too, Mac," she said quietly.

"Then you'll come?"

"If you're sure."

"Sure?" The fear was still there, but the excitement rushing in around it shattered it into tiny gleaming circlets like oil on stirred water. And she was laughing, a sound that started up the kid again.

"Meg," he shouted. "Hey, Meg."

She choked a little as she caught her breath.

"You got to call that kid something."

"I do," she admitted. "Remember what all the fellows used to try to hang on our Toby?"

"Jug," he replied.

"That's what I call him," she admitted very quietly.

"You have come a long way, Mrs. Maguire," he told her. Jug Maguire. If that wasn't an ace pilot's name, he had never heard one.

"When can you come?" he asked. "Don't wait around."

"The rent's paid until the first. "But I—"

"Hell, Meg, that's almost two whole weeks. God only took a week."

"You can't talk like that around Jug," she wailed.

"We'll work that out," he told her. Then, "Meg, hey, I really like this."

"Me too," she whispered. "Me too."

Mac paused in the door of the steak house letting his eyes adjust to the darkness so he could locate Len Frank. He was clear at the back, motioning to Mac with a stubby brown arm.

It took a minute for Mac to figure out what was going on. Grouped around that table with Len Frank were all the customers, the big ones, of the Flying Mick. Along with them was his lawyer, Jake Loman. All of them looked half drunk and it was only sundown.

"Sit, sit," Frank ordered, waving a glass he got from the skinny blond girl who had just set down a fresh pitcher of draft beer.

"Some kind of a celebration?" Mac asked, pulling in beside Frank.

"You might call it that," Jay Morgan said, beginning to slap his leg and laugh as if Mac had said something witty.

Mac lost track of the pitchers of beer. Even his steak wasn't enough to clear his head. And all the time they were talking, interrupting each other and shouting, selling him a bill of goods that he would never have thought of for himself.

"We'd be partners," Frank explained. "We'd buy that bastard Dobbs out. We always get first call on air time anyway so nothing would change except that you'd be running the business like in the old days."

"What makes you think he'd be willing to sell?"

"He might not see the light right away, but a few months of all those planes sitting on the runway with no work would bring him around."

"Is that legal?" Mac asked Jake Loman.

Jake poked at a potato shell on his plate. "Let's look at it this way, Mac. You've never worked for any of these men under contract. You can quit flying for them tomorrow if you want to. They have the same privilege not to ask you to. Dobbs might be able to drum up some little business here and there, but it would all have to be outside this valley. Among your friends, there's almost twenty-five miles of rice fields here at this table."

Mac nodded, not sure whether it was this harebrained scheme or the beer making him light-headed.

"The shop has to change its name," Jay warned, leaning toward Mac.

"What for?" Mac challenged.

"The Flying Mick, Inc.," Jay explained, roaring at Mac's sudden change of expression. "You're the Mick and we'd be the Inc."

That sounded like something Mac could drink to.

Then he remembered Meg's voice. "Me too. Me too."

"I got some announcing of my own," he said. "You remember when we lost Toby." The words got out. He even thought that maybe nobody noticed how hard they were to say as he went on quickly. "Well his baby came and it's a boy." He had to keep talking rapidly into that confused silence. "Meg and me, my wife, Meg, have been talking. She's bringing him out here, like in June."

Thank God for Jay Morgan. He broke the spell and in a way that everybody could handle. "Curtains at the Flying Mick," he shouted. "In that scabby old trailer, curtains."

"Only for a while," Mac told him. "I'm going to put up a little place on that lot . . ."

There was a lot of talk about the lot and who would do a decent job of getting a house up. There was at least one more pitcher of beer before they moved to the back room. Al set up a poker game. Mac lost a couple of hundred and won about the same. His head would have to be a lot clearer before he figured that out.

In the end Mary herself threw them out by threatening to call Sheriff Prentice. He remembered trying to get the truck out of the parking lot, which seemed to have sprouted a number of poles and walls that hadn't been there when he drove in.

Mostly he remembered getting halfway down that twenty-mile stretch of road between Blakeslea and the Flying Mick and having to pee so bad that he pulled over on the shoulder.

The moon was a left-handed melon rind and there wasn't a cloud in the sky anywhere. There was loose dust there by the truck when he finally got his zipper down. If he had ever been able to write his name in piss, this ought to be the night. He got most of the way through Flying and the big M for Mick when he ran out.

A night owl like the one that stayed around the hangar at the Flying Mick was complaining of the brightness of the night. He was too sleepy to go on, and anyway, when he woke up, he'd be able to add that "Inc." to make it legal.

When he wakened it was with a start. He was ice cold. That chill that comes just before dawn had almost frozen him there at the wheel of his truck. It wasn't light, but the promise of it was easing up the sky.

Jesus Christ. His men would be reporting within the hour. They'd be looking for those schedules he had left on his desk in the trailer. He hit the starter on the truck a couple of times before the motor turned over.

Another hour and there would be traffic on this road, pilots on their way to work, the ground crew pulling in with their lunches to get the nurse rigs ready. He had to get there in time to open up that shop like it was any other day. He was still drunk as a lord, but the road belonged to him at this hour. Hell, it wasn't a road at all but the longest runway in the history of aviation just lying there, waiting.

He gunned the truck and started with both windows of the truck all the way down. He sang at the top of his lungs every old bar song he'd ever learned in service.

He was raising such a ruckus that he didn't hear the other motor as he neared the Flying Mick. Only when he slammed to a stop by the office trailer did he realize that the throbbing sound he heard was Dobbs's P-39 taxiing out to the runway.

By the time Mac got the office opened and the schedules out for the pilots to pick up, Dobbs had apparently finished his instrument check. Mac heard the roar of the plane as Dobbs started down the runway, picking up ground speed for takeoff. He stepped outside and lit a fresh Camel, squinting into the morning to watch that devil go. The plane climbed steadily at a smooth, even angle.

He thought about how Dobbs must feel up there with that crochety machine fighting him for every inch, jammed into that narrow cockpit with the Allison engine screaming against his butt.

The plane was still climbing as Mac limped over to the house trailer. He laughed at the idea of curtains in it. How much had changed in an afternoon. Never mind that the jury hadn't had guts enough to call a clean shot. He would have Meg and that jug-eared kid and all those drunken ranchers behind him like a wall of rock.

Dobbs was clear out of sight by the time Mac let himself into the trailer to start his morning coffee.

The Flying Mick had been deserted when Dobbs pulled into the place a little before dawn. Mac wasn't around; there was only that pen of German shepherd dogs raising hell alongside the hangar as Dobbs locked up his car.

With his P-39 out on the runway, Dobbs crawled in, checked his tanks from old practice and hung the oxygen gear loosely around his neck.

Petcock on reserve, prop pitch forward, idle cutoff on "off," trim tabs neutral. "Okay," he whispered to himself.

"Prime the engine and lock down the primer," he crooned. "Jesus, you are one sweet crate."

When Dobbs hit the toe and heel starter on the floor the energizer began its long, slow howl. Then that goddamned clap of thunder that this plane was all about hit him square at the base of his spine and the fusilage began to tremble as if it had come alive.

Dobbs worked carefully, happily, through the checklist, then taxied slowly to the end of the strip, turned around and lined up. When he released the brake, the plane leaped forward heavily. Having stayed in control until the rudder took over, he knew he was home free. At a hundred and twenty ground speed he eased the nose wheel off and began to climb. At a hundred and seventy and still climbing the plane nestled into his hand like a warm bird.

The earth fell away steadily. Dobbs glanced down at the world he was suddenly on top of.

"Your comrades are pleased." He repeated the words with wonder, still able to hear Christa's voice behind the words. "What do you know, Stan Dobbs, you old bastard, what do you know?"

At ten thousand feet Stanley Dobbs snapped the mask over his face and flipped on his oxygen system.